AEVA

THE LAST HOPE

TORI C. LORE

Foxfield Publishing, P.O. Box 460203, Aurora, CO 80046

First Edition, 2021

Library of Congress Control Number: 2021902225

ISBN 978-1-954834-00-2 (paperback)

ISBN 978-1-954834-01-9 (ebook)

Printed in the United States of America

For the person who inspired this story

1

The space jet accelerated from the USS *Arcon* at full throttle. Its afterburner shimmered with shock diamonds as it headed toward the sister ship, the USS *Cana*. A few minutes into the flight, the jet made a peculiar sharp left away from its destination and in the direction of the asteroid belt, Sytka.

Almost an hour later the jet arrived in the asteroid belt and slowed down to avoid colliding with the scattered rocks. The pilot maneuvered around the asteroids with precision until he came upon the stranded cargo ship floating amid the rocks. The pilot shot a thermal imaging beam from his control panel at the ship as a precaution in case any survivors were on board. The cargo ship had been lost for 24-hours so he wasn't expecting any survivors, but to his surprise, the thermal laser picked up an object of pale heat radiating from the flight deck. The object was in a prostrate position on the floor of the ship and wasn't moving. The radiating heat was a clue that whoever it was, was still alive. For how long, he didn't know, and had no way of knowing, but there was no doubt he would attempt to extract this person. It might take an hour for a crew to show up and this person could be dead by then. Besides, it wasn't in his nature to let someone die or have someone else save the life he was already there to do.

The pilot radioed the sistership. "This is Captain Teschner. I've arrived at Sytka per directive."

"Captain, what is your report?" the *Cana* operator asked.

"I've located Cargo Ship 24 on the edge of Sytka. It appears to be abandoned. I'm reading a thermal profile from the flight deck. Going in."

"Do not enter C24, Captain. It's too dangerous. We only need you to confirm the ship is stranded. Please proceed to *Cana* immediately. A crew is on the way to extract the ship. Do not enter. I repeat. Do not enter. Over."

"I'm going in," he said.

There was a short pause before the operator spoke again. "Captain, I have orders you are to head to *Cana*."

There was no response from Teschner.

"Captain? Captain!"

Teschner ignored the directive and positioned his jet above the cargo ship, landing with a gentle thud over the emergency exit of C24. He deployed clamps to hold his jet down onto the ship. Once all was secured, he opened the floor door and climbed down into the ship. It was dark inside except for the green emergency lights along the walkway guiding him toward the flight deck. The oxygen level was low but there was still enough for him to find the body and return to his jet.

He wasn't far from the door into the flight deck; a few steps more and he would be there. The door was closed and next to it was a thumb print scanner. There wasn't a way for him to enter the flight deck without being a member of the crew and he didn't know the emergency code for the door either. He pounded on the door in frustration, at his bright idea that he could start off as a hero after having been fired from *Arcon*, from his last job as head captain with hopes of becoming general. To think he could still hold an established position on the sistership was foolish. He stopped pounding on the door when he noticed that the door latch looked a little off. He pulled on it and the door slid open.

He crossed the threshold into the flight deck. The deck wasn't very large and took him no time to locate the unconscious body lying face down to the right of the door. He rolled the body over. A female. She was pale and blue from lack of oxygen. He reached for a pulse on her neck and felt a subtle throbbing. He scooped her up into his arms and carried her out.

The USS *Cana* was familiar to Teschner. It was here he put in his flight hours after graduating from flight school. When he was done with schooling, he applied for the position of first officer for cargo transporting and worked on *Cana* for five years before he was promoted to captain. *Cana* would have been his new home if it wasn't for the raven-haired girl with the pale, gray eyes he'd met at the mask gala one year ago on *Arcon*. Her name was Maya Seymour and she was like no other he'd ever met. A captain in her own right, she led a rescue unit into one of the most dangerous districts on Pfore to extract imprisoned female naturals. Unlike her comrades, her missions were always successful with never a single death or injuries reported. Not only was she good at her job, she was a sight to behold with her pretty looks and fit and toned frame.

On the night of the masked gala, Maya was with some friends and bumped into Rowen on her way to the entrance. He'd turned to apologize but when he looked at her, he was lost for words. She too didn't say anything but only smiled, and that smile left an imprint on him. At the gala he asked for a dance and before he knew it, a year had past and he'd asked her to marry him.

She meant nothing to him now.

WHEN ROWEN ARRIVED on *Cana* a medical crew rushed to the unconscious female in the passenger seat. They put her on a stretcher and rolled her away even before he could step out of the cockpit. Approaching him was the placement resources personnel, Liz. "Welcome back, Teschner," she said, but not sounding too delighted to see him again. "Why don't we head to my office and work out the details of your new home."

Rowen sat down across from Liz at her desk and leaned back in his seat. On her monitor, she pulled up his file concentrating on the updates on his file. Crossing her arms, she said, "You got yourself into a bit of a mess."

"Look, if you're upset that I got the girl out of the cargo ship, you have every right to be, but I wasn't going to leave her there for dead."

"I'm not referring to the incident with C24. I was notified that you were heading here for a work-related transition, but I wasn't aware that you were banned from *Arcon* for misconduct and can no longer be allowed to fly. Your file was just updated with this information. The details are not provided, but you must've really screwed up."

"Yeah," was all he said.

"This makes it difficult for me to place you. *Cana* is the hub for medical equipment and medical data. It's our specialty and because you are grounded as a pilot there is really nothing I can give you that would be anything close to what you have experience in. Why did you choose *Cana* of all places?"

"I didn't choose *Cana*. It was chosen for me."

"*Cana* isn't for someone like you. I have authority to transfer you somewhere else. Do you have anything in mind? Stromnair? I can have you shipped there once I have an available pilot. We're shorthanded at the moment."

"The rain on Stromnair gives me headaches."

"There's Snazatriptan for it."

"Snaz makes me groggy and the depression can be unbearable."

"What about Taonos?"

"Never been there but heard there's not enough oxygen. Besides, I'm not very familiar with their ecosystem. Don't want to chance my one and only choice."

"What about—"

"Earth?"

"Earth is not in our direct planetary system. Plus, it is closed to immigrants at the moment and won't be opened for some time. I was saying, what about Pfore?"

Rowen glared at Liz and she knew Pfore was out of the question. Pfore was home to the Ryths, the alien species he loathed for a couple of reasons. Ryths were using female naturals as baby incubators for their kind. Initially, he thought it couldn't be possible. Ryths laid a single hard-shell egg for every birth, so how was it even possible for a human uterus to house a hard egg? He learned it was possible while on an operative to rescue a group of captured female naturals. In the group was a pregnant woman carrying a Ryth egg in her womb. After she was brought to safety, a C-section was done immediately to remove the egg. Had the egg been allowed to mature, it would have opened inside her, killing her and the Ryth baby. Ryths used a procedure to remove the egg before it hatched inside the female natural, and because he was not a scientist or a physician, he didn't know what it was.

The other reason was Krane Altontaur, the Ryth incumbent general of the mothership, USS *Arcon*. The position of general was supposed to be given to Rowen on his return from his last mission. However, Altontaur schemed his way into the position and was inaugurated two weeks before Rowen's return. Not only did Altontaur take the position from him, Altontaur also blackmailed his wife into marriage. Rowen had been married to Maya for three months when he left on the mission. On his return, he learned Altontaur had copulated with his wife and tagged her with a septum piercing, a sign that she belonged to the general. It was the Ryth way of showing ownership. Once owned, it wasn't easy to be unowned. Maya was conveniently tagged on the day he returned from his mission. That same day, he was forced to annul the marriage and resign his position. To top it off, Altontaur exiled him from *Arcon* and sent him to *Cana* as a gesture of "kindness" for his excellent work, but it was a bunch of bullshit. The Ryth general was protecting himself from the Federation.

Liz let out a loud yawn. "All right. Pfore's out. Your home will be here for now. Jobwise, I don't have too many positions open because most the workers here—GENs, were made specifically for their specific jobs, so the only position I can give you at the moment is Biomedical Equipment Maintenance Technician. It's a level two position in medical maintenance. Generally, maintenance techs are GEN-only positions because of the long hours and the volunteer requirement. I'll do what I can to reduce your hours and we'll talk volunteer in a bit here. Any questions so far?"

"No."

"I'm not sure if you're aware but naturals in GEN positions are required to be under contract. This is just how we keep track of naturals coming through. You'll be evaluated every year. At that time, you can renew your contract or transfer to a different position, if one is available. You can also leave *Cana* all together. If you choose to leave *Cana*, keep in mind that *Arcon* is not an option. If you breach your contract at any time during your service, policy is, you'll be banned from *Cana*, so be very careful. One more ban after that and it's out of my hands. The Federation will then decide your fate, and there's a possibility they'll send you to the sun to roast." Liz pushed a tablet over to him. "Please sign the contract. I'll submit your information over to medical maintenance so they can expect you first thing tomorrow." Rowen signed the contract and pushed the table back to Liz. "As I mentioned earlier, level two employees are required to volunteer. Our main volunteer areas are cargo loading, unloading, and shipment of our medical equipment and supplies. Since you can't leave *Cana*, we have a dilemma. I wasn't given enough time to prepare a volunteer position for you, so I'll have to get back to you on that."

"Fine with me."

Liz typed on her keyboard and then touched the screen to close his file. "You're all set. I've sent for an assistant to show you to your cabin. He should be here shortly." Just as she finished talking, a buzz came at the door letting them know the assistant was there.

T hree days later, Rowen was back in Liz's office. A volunteer position was available, and she wanted to go over it with him. Sitting across from her, he watched as she pulled up his file on the screen. As she was about to explain the volunteer position an image of a gray-haired woman appeared over his file. "Liz, is Mr. Teschner with you?" the gray-haired woman asked.

Liz glanced at Teschner who raised an eyebrow. "He's with me, Miriam. I'm setting him up for volunteer. What can I do for you?"

"I need you to cancel that and send him over to investigation immediately."

"Of course," Liz said to Miriam. The older woman didn't say anything else and disconnected. Liz looked at Rowen. "You heard what Miriam said. I'll walk you over."

"There's no need," Rowen stood up. "I know where to go."

The investigation unit was on the same deck but at the far end of the ship. Miriam greeted him by the entry where he followed her in.

"Good to see you, Teschner. Have a seat." She gestured at the white leather sofa. Her office was more like a fancy suite. There was a comfortable seating area, a nook setup for cocktails, and a round table with cushioned chairs. "Admiral Johnston was supposed to join us but had a meeting to attend. Would you like something to drink? Bourbon?" she asked while he sat down on the sofa.

"Are you trying to make it easier for me to squeeze out whatever details I have of C24 and the girl?"

Miriam grinned. She was calm, a lot calmer than she sounded on the screen. She crossed her arms and stood behind the sofa across from him. The old lady was in top-notch shape for her age. Rowen guessed she was in her early sixties, though she could easily pass for a late twenty-some-thing if she didn't have gray hair.

Rowen knew why investigation asked for him. It was apparent they needed to question him, or reprimand him, or both, about removing the evidence on Cargo 24. He knew saving the female crew member would cause backlash from those in authority. They could throw him in jail for all he cared. He had nothing to live for. He missed the life he had. Everything he'd worked for was taken from him within a few hours. He didn't deserve it but there was little he could do with Krane Altontaur in power.

He would leave *Cana* after his one-year contract ended. By then, he'd hope to have some idea of where he'd like to live. Earth would have been a good choice but being that it was closed to outsiders, he would need to find a place similar to it.

"You must be wondering why you're here," Miriam said.

"I wasn't going to let her die," he said, sure of his conviction.

"I'm not going to berate you on saving 818 or your decision not to follow directives."

"No? Then just throw me in the brig. I'm done answering." He stood up to leave.

"I won't be doing that either."

"What do you want?"

"I need your help."

Rowen sat back down. He had expected Miriam to read him his rights, to see guards walk into her office, cuff him, and take him away. Instead, she needed—not wanted, but needed his help. "General Altontaur will deny it, I'm sure."

"It's a volunteer position and something the general doesn't need to know about."

"What kind of volunteer work are we talking about?"

Miriam sat down on the sofa across from him. "You saved 818's life, and I commend you for your heroic pursuit of a fallen human, or any living soul for that matter. Nevertheless, a part of me wished you had followed directives. I know you couldn't leave 818 to die. I wouldn't either, but we now have a problem. *Arcon* Investigation wants to interrogate her. They say it's not so much an interrogation but a Q&A session to clear up a few things. If they don't get their answers from the Q&A, they will take her to *Arcon* for the interrogation. Right now, she's not up to par for questioning. She's lost some memory of that event due to the Z-gas emitted into the chambers of the cargo ship. Dr. Emmit believes she's in a state of amnesia so if *Arcon* gets their hands on her—"

It occurred to Rowen that all this talk about *Arcon* and Altontaur wasn't making him feel any better. "Let them have her," he cut Miriam off. "I don't want anything to do with *Arcon*. In fact, I'd rather not volunteer for this if I have to deal with anyone from there."

"I can't let them have her. They'll turn her into a baby

incubator."

"Didn't know GENs could have babies."

There was hesitation before Miriam said, "She's a natural."

"What's a natural pretending to be a GEN?"

"It's a long story and now's not the time for it. Besides, that's not an issue at the moment. What I need is to get her memory back. If she can't answer *Arcon* agents because she doesn't remember anything, we'll lose another female natural. We can't lose another one."

Rowen didn't speak right away. He knew all too well what Ryths were capable of. He lost his ex-wife to one and she's probably carrying a Ryth baby right now while he was here finding his way around his new life. "What do you want me to do?" he asked after some thought.

"I need 818 to remember the details of that incident. Nothing is making sense to me and she is the only person that can clear it up. If you can pretend to be a friend and get close to her, we might get somewhere. Dr. Emmitt has taken her off her medications. He believes the combination of the Z-gas and medications are what's causing her memory loss."

"You want me to pretend to be a friend? You think she's better off talking to a complete stranger—someone she's never met, never even heard of?"

"Her current friends and co-workers are GENs. They don't understand human connection the way you and I do. I know it won't be easy, but you are charismatic, and I've known you to be excellent with people...and charming around the ladies."

Rowen laughed. "Don't stroke my ego. It's not working."

"We're in a dire situation here, Teschner. I was tossing and turning in bed trying to figure out what to do and then I find out you're back on *Cana*, and a lightbulb went on. It didn't take me very long to realize you were the perfect person for this job. What else would you be more interested in doing than simply spending time with a young lady?"

"You do know I was recently divorced."

"I'm sorry. It happens to the best of us. I hope you can put your grieving aside for just a few weeks and help me work through this."

Rowen didn't say anything.

"818 works on the Assembly Center floor in Data Processing and Analytics. I've told her department supervisor to expect you soon. There's one thing you should be aware of. If 818 seems agitated or confused, give her a few minutes to collect herself. Be patient with her. Don't get frustrated or raise your voice. Aside from the amnesia, she functions fine. Our main concern is her memory of the incident. *Arcon* Investigation will be here in a month, so I'll need her to be well enough to answer their questions. They're not going to be easy on her."

"It's not a guarantee I can get anything out of her, especially in a few weeks. What happens then?"

"You won't have to worry about that. You would have done your part, and we would have done all that we could do."

"I'll do what I can." He stood up. "Is there a name I can call her by?" he asked before turning to leave.

"Aeva."

He walked to the door and before leaving, Miriam said, "Before you go, I should tell you that 818 doesn't know she's a natural. I'd like to keep it that way." He stopped and turned to face her, frowning. "Ryths don't know either...not yet anyway. There's a possible chance that if they truly think she's a GEN, they won't take her. GENs are useless to them."

He turned and left.

4

Three years ago, when Rowen was a cargo pilot for *Cana*, he never had to go down to the Assembly Center where the GENs processed medical data. Now that he lived and worked in their environment, he was beginning to understand the intricacies of their daily lives. Genetically Engineered Naturals were similar to artificial intelligence in that they were designed for specific duties and responsibilities. Their DNAs were manipulated in ways that allowed them to function with minimalist natural human behavior. This was to make sure work was a priority. They were not without human emotions or characteristics, on the contrary. GENs enjoyed parties and drinking, traveling, and meeting people. They were allowed to date and become couples, but they were not allowed to marry. They were designed without reproductive systems so they cannot reproduce. They knew that they were genetically altered humans, and their purpose was to aid in the advancement of humankind. Strict protocols have been placed to keep them in line and so far, within the last decade, there have been no extreme deviations. GENs were a quiet and reserved bunch. They could be loud when partying but again, they were made to work and so they don't often care to party hard or very much. They knew their schedules and duties and it was rare that any of them would get out of line. They enjoy working long hours and do so without minimal side effects.

Rowen was told that Tish Carinton would introduce him to 818. When he reached the front desk of the Assembly Center, the receptionist said, "You must be here to see Mrs. Carinton?"

"That's correct."

"She's expecting you, but at the moment she's down the hall in DPA. If you wait a few minutes I can call her up here."

"DPA?"

"Data Processing and Analytics."

"Gotcha. If it's not a bother, I don't mind heading down there."

"Go right ahead."

Rowen thanked the receptionist and went on his way. As he approached the door to the processing room, he could hear a women's voice talking as if to a child who got in trouble.

"I'm your boss and you do as I say!" the voice boomed, then demanded, "Tell me, who is your boss?"

Another voice—a much quieter one replied, "You are."

"That's right. I'm your boss and you do what I tell you to do, not what anyone else tells you. Understood?"

"I understand, but it was Meerton who told me—"

"Did you not hear me? I am your boss and you are only to do what I tell you to do! What part of that do you not understand? How stupid are you? Everything comes through me in this department. I approve everything! I am the senior director of this department and I sign off on all requests before they are sent off. You were in the wrong to allow Meerton to sign off. You are not the boss. He is not the boss. I AM. I am your boss and you do as I say."

"I know."

"You don't know, otherwise you wouldn't have sent the request without my approval."

"Meerton said it was an emergency and that you would okay it."

"Stop it with Meerton! It's not so much his fault as it is yours. You were not to do as he told you. Not a damn thing. How many times do I have to repeat myself? You are to do only what I say. If I don't know about it, you don't do it. You don't send any requests unless I approve it. Period. Get that through your thick skull. I. AM. YOUR. BOSS."

There was silence that followed. The other person kept quiet while the boss continued.

"What you did was wrong, Aeva. Very wrong. I will write you up for this lapse of judgement. Don't let it happen again because there won't be another warning." The boss turned around and took a few steps toward the door when she saw Rowen with his arms crossed, leaning against the wall inside the door. "Well, what a surprise." The boss beamed with a huge smile. "You must be looking for my employee, Aeva. I'm Tish Carinton, Senior Director of Medical Data Processing and Analytics." She held her hand out.

Rowen shook it. "Rowen Teschner."

"Mr. Teschner, I'm so sorry you had to hear our conversation. I had to teach Aeva a lesson. She isn't the brightest GEN, as you'll learn. She made a terrible mistake and needed to be chastised. Fortunately, it was something harmless. It could have been worse. Come on over and let me introduce you to her."

Rowen wanted to say, "Maybe another time," but Tish was keen on the introduction grabbing him by the elbow and pulling him toward Aeva's cubicle.

"Mr. Teschner, meet my GEN employee, Aeva, or 818 as we naturals also know her by." Tish spoke as if the incident just seconds ago never happened.

Aeva removed her headset and stood up. The workers seated in the cubicles next to hers had their headsets on and appeared to be consumed by their work. A few of them looked up but returned to their tasks.

Tish continued. "She's our level one processor which means she inputs information we receive from the Federation into our databases. It's an easy job, but somehow it's difficult for her."

Aeva managed to put on a weak smile. "Nice to meet you," she said politely, but Rowen heard the faint quaver in her voice.

"Same," he said then added, "Look, maybe we can do this another time?"

Aeva opened her mouth to speak but Tish interrupted. "No, no. It's all right. You're here already. Why don't the two of you go into the office next door. It's empty in there for now."

Rowen looked from Aeva to Tish. "Are you sure?" he said to Tish.

"I wouldn't want to screw up the investigation. Take all the time you need. If Aeva gets difficult, yell at her. That'll put her in place."

In the office, Rowen sat behind the desk while Aeva took a seat in front of it. Rowen leaned forward with his hands folded on the desk. Aeva sat leaning back with her arms crossed over her chest. She kept her eyes away from him, glancing anywhere but him.

"Is that how she always is?" he asked, not meaning to get involved even though it bothered him how Aeva was treated.

"Can we talk about what you're here for?" Aeva sounded irritated, or maybe it was embarrassment.

"Sure. Let's talk about the C24 incident."

"You're a little late. I've already said everything to investigation. Miriam was her name."

"Right. Okay."

"Teschner is it? I've heard of you. You're from the mothership, USS *Arcon*. You're the captain of the Absolution Rescue Mission Team."

"I didn't know you knew."

"I read the Federation News. I'm not supposed to, but I find it interesting. There's a lot of stuff about you there... about the missions on finding missing naturals. No one cares about the news here. Miriam said something about *Arcon* Investigation coming here to interrogate me. I'm guessing that's you?"

He was surprised at how much she knew about his old job. If they were in a different situation, a less pressured one, he'd asked her why the intrigue, but it wasn't the time and place. "I'm not with *Arcon* Investigation," he said.

"If you're not with them, what are you here for?"

"Miriam asked me to talk to you in hopes that I can help with getting your memory back."

"I don't have a problem with my memory."

Rowen realized this was going to be tougher than he'd thought. Aeva was no robot, not that he thought she was anything close to one, he just didn't realize she was so human. And it's not that he didn't think she wasn't human, but she looked so much like a GEN in her green jumpsuit and short hair, trimmed to chin-length. All the female GENs had the same jumpsuits on and the same short hair. He'd never guess she was a naturally born human.

"Like I said, I've already told Miriam everything," she said after Rowen didn't respond.

"I'm not going to ask the questions Miriam already asked. You can tell me whatever you want, no pressure." This time she didn't respond so he continued. "I kind of want to spend time together to talk. That's it. Just talk."

She still didn't say anything.

"How about we do lunch tomorrow?" he asked. "I only meant to introduce myself this morning. Have to head back to work and I'm sure you do too. What do you say?"

Before Aeva answered, a man opened the door and peeked in. They both turned to face him. "Aeva—oh—" the man glanced at Rowen then back to Aeva. "You're busy...can I come in for a sec? It won't take long."

Rowen stood up then. "Actually, we're done. I just wanted to touch base with Aeva."

"You sure?" the man said.

"Yep." Rowen turned to Aeva who stood up too. "I'll come get you for lunch tomorrow?"

"Sure," she said.

The man at the door stepped into the room and as Rowen walked past him the man reached out his hand for a handshake. "I'm Meerton, by the way. Meerton Slandsome. I'm the Medical Data Transfer and Storage Senior Supervisor, and Aeva's direct boss. You look familiar. Have we met?"

"I doubt it. Rowen Teschner." Rowen shook Meerton's hand.

"*The* Captain Teschner of the Absolution Rescue Mission group? I know who you are. I've heard great things about you. It's a pleasure to finally meet you."

"You as well," Rowen said with a nod then left quickly.

Out the door, he paused on the other side and heard their conversation. "What's Captain Teschner talking to you about?" Meerton asked.

"The investigation."

"He's with the *Arcon* investigation team now?"

"He's with Miriam."

"An *Arcon* pilot on a *Cana* team?"

"I guess so."

"Hmm...that's fishy. Anyhow, I just wanted to tell you, I'm so so sorry. I just found out what Tish said to you. She had no right to treat you like that. It was my fault. I forgot to tell her and then lost track of things..."

That was all Rowen heard because the conversation faded out as he walked away.

5

The next day, Rowen went to the Assembly Center to take Aeva to lunch. The receptionist wasn't at the front desk, so he went straight to Aeva's cubicle. He expected to see her, but she wasn't there. A couple of processors were at their cubicles with their headphones on and their heads bent down deep in their work. He ran his hand through his hair. *Did she forget?*

Down the hall he heard two people talking and made his way toward the voices. As he got closer one voice sounded like Aeva's. The other was a man's voice. Rowen stopped at the door briefly. He didn't want to interrupt them, so he waited.

"Thanks for verifying those files for me, Jared," Aeva said to the man named, Jared.

"Any time," Jared said.

"So...um, talk to you later?"

"Um-hm."

"Before I go, I wanted to ask, did you want to go together to the Century Ball next weekend? I thought maybe because it was the 200th anniversary celebration of our species out in space that it might be fun to go together."

"Sorry, something came up last minute."

"What came up?"

"Work related stuff."

"Will it take all night?"

"I'm not sure how long it'll take but I don't want to disappoint you."

"Maybe we can do something the day after? I'm free all day."

"I'm pretty busy all weekend actually."

Aeva paused for a second. "I understand. Maybe we can hang out another time?"

"Yeah."

"See you later," she said, disappointed.

Aeva spun out of the door so fast she slammed into Rowen's chest. He steadied her with his hands on her waist while she held onto his arms for balance. Within seconds she composed herself, stepping away from him. "What are you doing here?" she asked.

"I thought we were doing lunch."

"That's right!" Her cheeks flushed.

The cafeteria was a big round area a floor above the Assembly Center. It served a variety of hot and cold food and beverages. The seating areas were clean and quiet for the most part. They grabbed their food trays and sat down at a corner booth.

"You seem to be doing well," Rowen said while holding a fork full of salad near his mouth.

"Better than yesterday, I suppose." Aeva twirled the spaghetti with her fork slowly as though thinking about something.

"Meerton's your boss, not Tish?"

"He's my direct boss. I report to him. Tish is Meerton's boss, so technically, she's my boss too."

"If Meerton's your direct boss then don't you do as he asks?"

"You would think."

"What made Tish so angry yesterday?"

"Meerton had asked me to send a request for a medical kit to a medical student on Taonos. When the student received the kit, he e-mailed a thank you to Meerton and Tish, and because she wasn't aware of the request, she flipped out.

"It's normal procedure to send medical students the medical kits. Tish knows the count of the medical student who are given kits and knows how many kits go out. It just so happened that this student didn't receive his. He was accidentally marked as having received it, but we couldn't track down the shipping—because there wasn't one. Plus, our inventory showed an extra kit which would have been the student's. Tish was in a meeting at the time the kit needed to go out and Meerton said he would notify her once she came out of her meeting. He'd forgotten to mention it to her until she received the thank you e-mail from the student. She needed someone to yell at and she'd never yell at Meerton so I got the brunt of it. I think she also hates me. I'm not her expectation of what a GEN is supposed to be. She knows I'm a defect and medicated and because I've been taken off my meds, I think she thinks I'm going to go crazy on her so she's trying to kick me out of her department."

"Sounds like the issue should have been between her and Meerton."

"She wanted the opportunity to write me up." Tears lined Aeva's eyes and she blinked them away.

"What happens if you get written up or get on her bad side again?"

"I'd get sent to roast. I don't have the option to move to a different department. I'm specifically made for my position. It's all I know to do. She knows that, and she knows that if I'm found faulty or damaged beyond repair—as they call us defects; if we don't do our work the way we're made to do them, we simply don't exist."

"Gotcha."

Rowen finished his salad and saw that Aeva was now moving the spaghetti around on her plate with the fork. She hadn't taken a single bite of it.

"How old are you, Rowen?" she asked. It took him by surprise. "Can I call you Rowen, Mr. Teschner?"

"Sure. Are you going to eat your food?"

She twirled a few noodles onto her fork and ate it. Rowen watched her and grinned. "I like Rowen better. It's not so formal, you know?" she said after swallowing her food.

"I agree."

"So?"

"Twenty-eight."

"I was close." She smiled. "A girlfriend and I made a bet about your age. I said you were twenty-seven. She said thirty-two. Her reason was because you were an elite pilot and most pilots can't make it as an elite until they're at least thirty."

"True for the most part. What was your reason?"

"I thought you were one of those geniuses who moved ahead of the ranks because you had mad skills."

"I like your reason better."

"I do too." She put a forkful of spaghetti in her mouth.

"This is actually really good." She twirled another forkful and stuffed it in her mouth.

"You've never had spaghetti?"

"It never looked appetizing. I guess I should try more things."

"Why this time?"

"Thought it'd be a short lunch. Didn't think we'd have much to talk about and saw no problem with throwing the spaghetti away without feeling guilty."

He didn't say anything, but there was a grin on his lips.

"I wonder why they chose you to talk to me of all people. You're a captain and not just any captain. You do those missions that no one can do. I can't possibly imagine why you'd be interested in talking to an ordinary GEN."

"You're not ordinary. You survived the hijack. During my time as captain, I've never heard or experienced anything remotely close to that. You managed to survive and send an S.O.S. How were you able to do something like that when all your comrades couldn't make it past the gas?"

Her face got serious and she put her fork down. "Like I've told Miriam, I don't know, and I can't remember."

"Bullshit."

She looked at him in shock. "I get it. You think I had something to do with it. You think I'm working with the rebels." She stood up.

"That's not what I think." He stood up as well. "I'm trying to help. If you just sit, I can explain."

"Explain what? That I'm hiding something? That I know who was behind it?"

"No. You had nothing to do with it. Just take a seat and let me explain—"

"I'm done," she said and walked off.

He ran after her and caught up to her before she got on

the elevator. "Aeva, I'm not here to accuse you of anything. There's no hidden agenda. I promise."

She looked at him for a long time, assessing his truthfulness. "I have to get back to work and you should too."

"Fine, but let's talk some more later today. What do you say I pick you up and we go for a drink and walk around the greenhouse chamber?"

She agreed.

6

L ater that evening, Rowen knocked on Aeva's cabin door. She opened the door wearing a knee-length floral print dress. She had on pink lipstick that matched the color of the flowers on her dress. Her hair was short, but she had bangs and they were clipped to the side with a sparkling hairpin. "Hi," she said smiling and looking him up and down.

He looked down at his black t-shirt and gray slacks. He wasn't dressed half as nice as she was and felt embarrassed. "Maybe I should change into something nicer."

"You look perfect. I like dressing up every chance I get so don't worry about it."

"You don't go out often?"

"Not often. I've gone to the bar alone a few times, but I seem to attract the wrong guys."

"What kind of guys?"

"Maintenance techs. Ugh, I can't stand them. They're always dirty and stinky and they never say much."

Rowen scratched his head. "I hate to tell you this but I'm a maintenance tech."

"You're a captain."

"I was discharged from my position and banned from *Arcon*. Shall we head to the bar?"

"Wait, you're not a captain anymore?"

"I'd rather not talk about my life and focus on you—on your memory."

"Fair enough," she said.

They walked toward the cafeteria where the evening bar was open. There wasn't anyone else around. Rowen ordered a beer while Aeva ordered a cosmopolitan. "Is it always this empty around here?" he asked.

"It's a workday and a lot of people work through the night."

"Would you be doing the same if I wasn't here?"

"If I was a normal GEN, yes. Since I'm a defect, I'm not allowed to work extremely long hours."

"Do you feel and think any differently off the medications?"

"If by different you mean having my memory back, no. I never lost my memory. I went unconscious due to the effects of the Z-gas. The memory I don't have and can't possibly have was during my unconsciousness. I remember everything before going into the cockpit. After that, things got fuzzy. If you mean by being more conscious of who I am...I think so. I feel oddly deep emotions like...like..." She paused to find the words. "...I'm not sure how to describe them. I get these feelings that come in waves...no, not waves. Spurts. They come in spurts and sometimes stronger than others."

"Deep emotions as in a craving or an urge?"

"No. It's like I want to touch and be touched, to hug and be held. I want to be intimately and emotionally close. What do you think this could be?"

Rowen was silent, thinking her words through.

"How would you describe love?" she asked without giving him much time to answer her previous question.

"I'd describe it as a strong feeling of affection for someone."

"Hmm...doesn't seem to fit that. It feels more like a vulnerability than a strong feeling. It's not love."

"There could be vulnerability in loving someone. The thing is love is complex. You've been in a relationship, haven't you?"

"I have but I've never had these emotions that's why this is so confusing to me."

"How close have you gotten in a relationship? Can you marry?"

"We're not allowed to, but we also don't have an interest in spending the rest of our life with one person."

"I see. What happens if a GEN wants to, due to a defect?"

"I've never thought about that. I wouldn't know what would happen, but my guess would be that they'd be given medication to make them forget about it."

"Is that similar to your situation? Were you on medication to make you forget?"

"The medications helped me focus, not to mess with my memory. What are you insinuating?"

"Nothing—"

"Are you saying I might not have all my memory due to the medications and now that I'm off the medications, I should have memories I wouldn't have had?"

"Possibly."

Aeva furrowed her eyebrows thinking over what he'd said. "You really think with being off my medications I should remember more of the incident?"

"That's what Miriam is hoping for."

"Do you realize how scary that sounds to be bombarded with a slew of memories all at once?"

"I could imagine and wouldn't wish it on anyone. Miriam and your doctor would have discussed any side effects beforehand so there's nothing to worry about."

"Can we talk about something else? All this talk about memory, medications, and being a defect is depressing."

"Sure. Let's see..." he said, thinking. There wasn't much else he knew to talk about.

"What do you think about the 200th century anniversary of humankind in outer space?" she asked when he couldn't come up with anything.

"It's pretty amazing."

"Isn't it?" A smile spread across her lips. "I'm elated knowing how far humanity has come. And I know I'm not a natural born, but I'm still human in many ways, and knowing how far our species has come means a great deal to me."

He smiled too. There was an innocence about her that warmed him, yet at the same time, made him feel sorry for her. She deserved better from the people who controlled her life. "I'll go with you," he said.

His words caught her off guard. "What?"

"The Century Ball. I'll go with you."

Her mouth dropped open. "No way."

"I'd like to be your date."

"Not because you feel sorry for me?"

"I don't—" he began. Aeva squinted at him like she still didn't believe him. "Why would you think that?"

"I have a feeling you heard me ask a co-worker to the ball."

"Maybe I did, but I can still go with you, can't I? Look, I haven't been to a century ball myself. It's a privilege and I can't imagine anyone turning it down. I genuinely want to go with you. The question is, will you go with me, a maintenance tech?"

Aeva laughed, then said, "I'd love to."

They left the bar to the greenhouse chamber. Inside the chamber were leafy bushes and shrubs with large arching leaves. Saplings of different heights and thickness scattered the room. The ground was grassy and giant mossed rocks sat among wildflowers. Birds chirped and sang among themselves with the sound of a waterfall nearby.

They moved further in and were greeted with tall trees forming a canopy covering the glass ceiling and hiding the stars. The vastness of the chamber felt like a real rain forest. It was humid and reminded Rowen of his vacation to Stromnair. But unlike Stromnair, it wasn't raining all the time. The chamber was a controlled environment.

They strolled through the chamber on the walkway while Aeva explained how GEN relationships and dating life worked. There were rules and guidelines they were to abide by, but the rules and guidelines were often not followed. There wasn't anyone in charge to make sure the rules were followed. But even if there were someone in charge, most GENs would not report the rule-breakers due to the fear of being called a tattler or a liar if rumors were to spread. It was better to take your losses and move on.

After Aeva shared what she knew about the dating life and relationships of GENs, she said to the ex-captain. "I seem to know nothing about you, Rowen. I know you're only doing your job, but I can't help being curious about who you are. Tell me one thing about you that isn't work related."

"There's not much to me, really," he said, then changed the subject. "I've been wondering though, and I know you don't want to talk about it, but I have one question about the

C24 incident that I'm curious about. You don't have to answer if you don't want to. The thing is, when I came looking for you and tried to get into the flight deck, the security lock was disabled requiring the emergency code to open. I was able to slide the door open by pulling the door latch. The latch should have been secured. You would have been the only person who would still be conscious enough to disable it unless someone else was there with you who disabled it."

"The pilot disabled the latch. He was alive when I made it to the cockpit door from the back, but he died soon after. The gas was much stronger in the cockpit than in the back and I'm guessing that's why I went unconscious after the S.O.S. Just in case you were wondering, the pilot and I were not working together."

"Who sent the S.O.S?"

A woman cleared her throat behind them, and they turned around. It was Tish Carinton and she was standing next to a man. "Mr. Teschner." She ignored Aeva and looked at Rowen with a wide smile. "How's the investigation going?"

"Going well, thank you."

"Let me introduce you to my husband, Richard. He was the chief operations officer of Medical Information Technology for thirty years having recently retired a year ago."

"Great meeting you," Rowen said and shook Richard's hand.

"We were taking our daily stroll when I thought it was you and Aeva I saw. You haven't had to yell at her yet, have you? Sometimes it can be difficult to get things out of her if you're not abrasive enough."

"You must be mistaking Aeva for someone else because she's been an immense help in the investigation."

"Really? I'm surprised. She's not the brightest—"

"You must not know her very well. Anyhow, I apologize, but we have other priorities we must get to." He turned to Tish's husband. "It was a pleasure to meet you, Mr. Carinton."

When they were out of the greenhouse chamber, Rowen said to Aeva. "Don't believe anything she says about you."

Aeva's face was bright pink. "You didn't have to do that." She looked away from him and bit down on her lower lip. "I better go."

She turned to leave, and he didn't go after her.

7

The next couple of days, Rowen was off work and took the time to catch up on a few things he wasn't able to since arriving on *Cana*. He'd spent some time thinking about what he wanted to do and where he wanted to be after his one year as a medical maintenance technician. Being reduced to a level two worker from an elite position was like being thrown in jail. His duties were to clean the currently-in-use machines after they were worked on by GEN levels three and four and to make sure the new machine counts were correct. Time with Aeva was more exciting than this, but he'd rather be flying or on missions than either.

There were other starships and planets that General Altontaur didn't rule over where he could resume as captain. These exoplanets were a little farther away on the outskirts of Messier Thirty-one. They didn't have the funding and support of the Federation, but they were part of the system, nevertheless. He needed access to the Federation's database to locate these planets. At the moment the only access was through the placement resource personnel, Liz, and his gut told him she would never allow it. She played by the rules. If he could be captain again, he'd find a way to destroy Altontaur.

Back at work after his two-day off, he went to a lunch meeting with Miriam and Admiral Johnston to go over Aeva's progress. There wasn't much progress, but he did relay the information about the pilot and the disabled latch allowing access into the cockpit. This ruled out any rebels from outside entering Cargo 24, but it still didn't answer what the motive was or why Aeva was the only one who survived. The pilot was a natural too.

That evening, he tried to reach Aeva to spend a few minutes talking to her to see how she was doing. As much as he tried calling her, she wouldn't answer. He went to her cabin and knocked on her door, calling out her name a few times. She didn't open her door or acknowledge she was inside. He gave it a rest and decided to check back tomorrow.

At the Assembly Center the next day, the receptionist told him Aeva was in a mandatory meeting and wasn't sure when she'd be done. "What about tomorrow. Is she free for lunch?" he asked just to make sure he wasn't going to be wasting his time.

"She's free tomorrow."

Tomorrow came, and he showed up at the Assembly Center a few minutes before Aeva's lunch time. "I'm here to have lunch with Aeva," he said.

"Let me call her." The receptionist began dialing Aeva's extension.

"I can grab her," he insisted.

"She's asked me to call her if anyone wants to visit."

"I'm not visiting. We've been working on the investigation."

"I'm sorry. She said no one." The receptionist continued watching the screen, waiting for Aeva's face to show up. A few seconds passed and nothing. "She's not at her desk. Let me call her over the intercom." The receptionist clicked a button and spoke into the microphone attached to her headset. "Aeva, you have a visitor at the front desk."

A minute passed and Rowen asked the receptionist to call again. Two minutes passed and no Aeva. "Are you sure she's in today?"

"She's here. I saw her earlier."

"Can I have her schedule?"

"I can't do that. Let me try the intercom one more time."

This time Aeva appeared on the screen. "Give me five minutes and I'll be right out," she said.

Rowen paced the floor, hands on hips. He wondered why he was so determined to help Miriam. He didn't have to try so hard. He could do a half-assed job and move on. There was nothing Miriam could do to him. Sure, she'd lose Aeva to the Ryths but she was one in thousands. He didn't need to deal with Aeva's stubbornness.

"Excuse me, Mr. Teschner."

Rowen was deep in thought and didn't see Miriam's assistant walk up to him until she spoke. "I'm sorry to bother you, but Miriam would like you in her office right now."

Rowen looked from the assistant to the receptionist. "Two more minutes," the receptionist said.

"Mr. Teschner, it can't wait," said the assistant.

"Let me have a few minutes with Aeva," he said to the assistant.

"It's an urgent matter, sir."

Rowen was infuriated and said harshly, "Give me a minute with Aeva. Just one damn minute."

The assistant swallowed and stayed quiet.

Two minutes passed. Then another. And another.

"How long has it been?" Rowen asked the receptionist.

"Seven minutes."

"Can I just go down there and say a few words to her?"

"No."

Rowen sighed. "Fine. Tell her I'll contact her."

"Will do," the receptionist said.

Rowen was going to rip Miriam a good one for demanding his presence. He entered her office and opened his mouth to speak but she was faster. "Two ships from *Arcon* landed on our runway thirty-seconds ago. One holds the *Arcon* Investigation team and the other, a slew of guards."

Astonished, he frowned and said, "I thought they said one month."

"They are trying to catch us off guard. We only picked up their signal when they crossed our shield. They were very secretive about it and it's because they don't want us to plan for their surprise visit. If they are here now, there is a possibility the interrogation will be tomorrow. Has Aeva brought up any new memory of the cargo incident?"

"I haven't been in contact with her since lunch with you and the Admiral. She's been a pain to find."

"Oh?"

"I was so close to seeing her today, except your assistant interrupted and asked me to come here."

"I better let you get back to her. I need you two to spend the rest of the afternoon together. I don't want her out of your sight until tomorrow. I've already notified her boss that you would be spending the rest of the afternoon with her for medical reasons."

"Should I bring her over to medical maintenance and have her watch me work? I'm not fortunate enough to take as much time as I need to fiddle in business that I have no real part in. If I breach my contract, I'm dead."

"Don't worry about your hours. I'll notify your boss of the situation. In fact, for your safety, I'll talk to Liz. I'll have her rescind your contract and reinstate you when this situation is over with. I'm hoping your part in this should only take a couple of months."

Rowen didn't say anything. He was thinking about the mess he unintentionally got himself into wondering if he could get himself out of it. Every step in the direction he was taking was leading him back to *Arcon*, and not in the way he wanted.

"Something on your mind?" she asked.

"Miriam, I'm not the guy for the job. I don't necessarily care for the situation. In fact, I'd have Aeva go to *Arcon* and let them do what they need done. They'll find she's a natural and use her to incubate their babies, but what's so bad about that? Soon they'll find a cure and they'll stop using humans. I'm just not ready to go the extra mile with this situation, especially that I'm being watched pretty carefully by those in authority."

"I know you're in a difficult position, but maybe this will change your mind." She paused longer than anticipated before continuing. "The late General Tom Cloudon of the USS *Arcon* is Aeva's father."

Rowen raised an eyebrow and opened his mouth to say something, but nothing came out. Miriam allowed him time to digest her words.

"I—" he began but couldn't find the words to describe his shock.

"This information isn't easy to digest. I had the same problem wrapping my head around it when I first learned about it."

When the shock settled, he said, "Didn't General Cloudon and his wife die from the Khardavirus pandemic which preceded the current virus that is now destroying the Ryths' reproductive system?"

"Yes, they died from the Khardavirus, but the general's wife was with child and the child survived. Before General Cloudon died, he put in a plan to save his baby. He used fake data to disguise his newborn daughter as a genetically engineered type two, also known as a GEN 2, to protect her. There were a few people he trusted this information to, but they too all died except for one person, his personal doctor. The doctor was a Ryth named Dr. Jamiah Batanthar. Dr. Batanthar died a year ago, but before he died, he spoke to me privately. He wanted to tell a natural he trusted of his secret because General Cloudon had been good to him and he felt he owed us this favor. He said the baby was given an emergency code to open special escape pods to return humans to earth if there should ever be a need for it. This code would only be used if all else fails with the human endeavors on the USS *Arcon* and the sister ship. The pods should only be used by natural humans. Genetically engineered humans wouldn't survive earth's environment.

"Very recently, I learned that Ryths have been trying to penetrate earth. As you are aware, they are in desperate need of female naturals with incubating capabilities and earth is full of them. They've had zero success so far in getting through earth's shield. Somehow, they've learned about the code. They don't know where this code is hidden, but they do know that it's hidden within a natural born. If they get a hold of Aeva and do an evaluation on her, they will find the code. The code is inside a chip about half a centimeter in diameter underneath her left shoulder blade. Dr. Emmit and I have falsified the scans when we submitted them to *Arcon* Investigation. In fact, her information has been falsified since her birth."

Rowen rubbed his eyes. "This must be the long story you were planning to tell me about."

"I wasn't planning to tell you at all, but with *Arcon* Investigation here, I didn't have a choice."

"Let me ask this. If she doesn't know she's a natural, I'm assuming she doesn't know about her father or the chip?"

"Correct."

"Do you plan to ever tell her any of this?"

"Not anytime soon."

"Why the fuck not? She seems capable."

"I know she's capable. The problem isn't because I don't want her to know. It's that if she knows, she will not be able to pretend to be a GEN well enough. It was a dangerous chance we took to get her off her medications. You've seen the changes."

"If she dies or gets sent to the sun, what happens?"

"Earth will be safe for a long time, but our existence— human existence in space, will die out."

"And you think it's worth protecting her?"

"I know it's worth it. We've come a long way, Teschner. We can't give it all up. We have to fight for our people, for everything we've done to create a place for us out here. It's not for nothing."

He remained silent.

"You of all people know how important it is to do what we do."

He clenched his jaw and looked hard at Miriam. "I'll help you on one condition. You will tell Aeva about who she really is. Not me."

"Deal."

8

The interrogation took place on the main floor of the ship. The room was set up with tables and chairs in a u-shape with a single chair in the center meant for Aeva. Rowen was not the first one in the room. To his surprise, the *Arcon* chief inspector, Tunjay Tharunbat, was already there with his team. Tunjay sat in the chair directly facing the center chair while four others sat to his left. He was busy chatting with the Ryth next to him and didn't see Rowen enter. A few minutes later, Miriam came in with Admiral Johnston. She sat next to Rowen while the admiral sat between her and Tunjay.

Aeva came in last. Rowen noticed that she looked despondent as if something hadn't gone well. She kept her head down, refusing to look at anyone including Rowen.

After his meet with Miriam yesterday, he was able to get through to seeing Aeva. He had cooled down by then and with the additional information he'd learned about her, he didn't want to come across irritated and irrational, so he kept his cool and proceeded with his duties. That evening, he noticed subtle changes to her that he couldn't pinpoint but they were enough for him to know that her medications were no longer aiding her. They went to dinner, but she didn't have a lot to say. She spent most the time observing him and the GEN waiters and staff at the restaurant. She wasn't in a talking mood, but she had a lot on her mind.

Rowen watched her make her way to the center seat wondering what could have happened to cause her to be in such a dispirited mood. *Did Tish say something to ruin her morning?*

"Let us begin," said Tunjay Tharunbat after Aeva took her seat. The talking amongst the group stopped and everyone turned their attention to him. "We are here for a Q&A with 818 regarding the Cargo Ship 24 incident. Does anyone have any questions or objections before we begin?"

No one spoke up so Tunjay continued. "818, you were the only survivor of Cargo Ship 24. Tell us your interpretation of the incident. Keep in mind—" he glanced at the others in the room, "—that survival is impossible with the Z-gas. No genetically altered human has ever survived this deadly poison so this will be interesting."

Aeva took a deep breath. "On the morning of take-off, the pilot, co-pilot, Simon 821, and I boarded Cargo Ship 24 en route to Taonos. This was my third volunteer duty and my first volunteer to Taonos. Nothing was unusual or out of the ordinary. Everything went smoothly until we reached the Sytka belt. The ship suddenly stopped. The lights went out and the emergency lights came on. I thought the engine went dead, but if so, the pilots would let us know.

"Within seconds a grayish purple gas came out from the vents. Simon 821 began coughing. I unbuckled my seat to see what I could do to help him, but he slumped over right as I got to him. I pulled his shoulders up and held his head back and that's when I saw blood out of his eyes, nose, and mouth. His eyes were rolled back, and he wasn't breathing. I began coughing myself but not loud and hard the way Simon 821 did before he died. I thought the same thing would happen to me, but my cough was only a tickling of my throat. I ran toward the flight deck. The co-pilot was dead, but the pilot wasn't at the time. He was groggy but was able to tell me what to do to send the S.O.S signal. He then crashed to the floor and stopped moving." She paused to collect herself. "That's when I lost consciousness."

"The pilot and co-pilot were naturals. The Z-gas does nothing to naturals. You are a genetically altered human, yet you withstood the Z-gas when they died from it. Want to explain that?" Tunjay questioned.

"I...I don't know how that could be."

"You're not telling the whole truth, are you?" The chief inspector didn't wait for Aeva to reply. "It's apparent you had a motive for the hijack. You must be part of the rebellion."

"I'm not."

"Do you have other motives?"

"No."

"I have a statement here from your boss, Tish Carinton, stating she heard you say to a co-worker that if there was an opportunity to escape *Cana*, you'd take it and never return. She claims you said you'd do anything to get away, including killing anyone who got in your way. The Z-gas was the perfect murder gas."

"I never said that, and I would never do anything to harm anyone. I don't even know what a Z-gas is or where to get it. Tish hates me. She wants me out of her department, and she'll do anything to get rid of me."

"Why is that?"

"I don't know. Why don't you ask her?"

"You were found unconscious in the cockpit. A GEN

should never be in the cockpit. The reason you were in the cockpit is because you were up to no good. It just so happened that your genius plan worked against you."

"I went to check on the pilots. What else was I to do?"

"You made sure the pilots were dead. It just so happened one of them had already sent the S.O.S."

"You have it all wrong. I sent the S.O.S."

"After you killed them. Now, the co-worker you talked to about your getaway also agrees with Tish."

"Who would that be?"

"901."

"Jared?" A look of surprise fell on her face. "That fucker," she said under her breath, but it was loud enough for everyone to hear.

Rowen saw the unshed tears glisten in her eyes. He knew she had a thing for the guy. She had told him that even though the dating rule was everyone was available to everyone she still found it difficult to go on a date with those she found attractive. She'd been eying Jared for a few months and finally found the courage to ask him to the Century Ball, only to be rejected.

"Yes, Jared," said Tunjay.

"It's true. I did tell them I wanted to get away, but I wouldn't hurt anyone. I don't have any reasons to put anyone in danger or to take their lives. I may have told Jared that if I could get away for a while, I'd travel space, but I'd always return to *Cana*, my home."

The room was quiet.

"We're still questioning you so don't deflect with your sentimental sorrows. It won't work."

"I've told you everything I know."

"In that case, we have no choice but to take you to *Arcon* for the full interrogation and further evaluation."

"That won't be necessary," Miriam stepped in. "You've got your answer and we've already provided the bloodwork you've requested."

"It's not enough. We have no other choice."

"You can't remove her from her *Cana*—from her environment. Doing so will agitate her beyond her normal capacity. She is a GEN made for this ship and must remain on this ship or she will not function properly."

"It's procedure, Detective Butterford."

Miriam raised her voice. "It's not normal procedure for a GEN. Aeva is an artificially engineered human designed specifically as a product of this ship to aid in the production of medical devices and products used by all as agreed by the Federation. Taking her away will weaken our efforts in this conglomerate. We've already suffered the loss of three people. We can't afford to lose another."

"I promise you, detective, she'll be returned safely and unharmed. You have my word."

"You cannot take her from her environment. She will not make it!" Miriam exclaimed, slamming her fist on the table.

Admiral Johnston, after having listened to the conversation finally spoke up. "Chief Tharunbat, Miriam has a point. Genetically engineered humans don't function at the same capacity as a natural human. Taking her to *Arcon* means you don't respect who she is or what it means to be human. You are endangering our kind, both natural and genetically altered, when your sole purpose is to find answers to an abandoned ship, disregarding ethics."

Tunjay took a deep, heavy breath and let it out through his nostrils. "As I've said, it is procedure and will only be for a short time. She will be returned safely, I assure you." He turned to the rest of group. "This session is adjourned. We will prepare to leave in a few hours."

Miriam stood up and went over to Rowen as the others began to exit the room. "I need you." She spoke so only he could hear. "Aeva needs to be hidden somewhere where she can't be found. I'll have a jet ready for you."

Rowen stood up and so did Miriam and Admiral Johnston. "I can't do that," Rowen said, looking from Miriam to the admiral and back to Miriam. "I'm grounded, remember?" He turned to where Aeva was sitting but she wasn't there. "Where's Aeva?"

"They must have taken her already. We need to find her!" Miriam exclaimed.

"Look, Miriam. I don't want to be a part of this—"

"None of us do."

"I can't put myself into this mess. Believe me, I don't agree with what the Ryths are doing, but it's not the fire I want to play with. Besides, I'm restricted, remember? Exiled. I'm not the person who can help you through this."

"I thought you agreed to help. Do you not see what she's worth?"

"To be honest, no. Earth is a great place I'm sure, but earthlings might be just as crazy as these Ryths. For all I care, they can have all the natural females they want."

"Unbelievable. I expected better from you, Teschner."

He shrugged. "Admiral," he said to the Admiral Johnston and proceeded to leave.

"Fine. We're done," Miriam said and took a couple of steps toward the exit. Before she was too far away, she stopped and added, "By the way, I didn't tell Liz to rescind your contract. I told her you refused to return to your job because it was beneath you. I had her enter a non-rescinding breach of contract in your file. Feel free to check. You have 24-hours to leave *Cana.*"

He went over to her. "Damn it, Miriam. Why the hell did you do that?"

"It was the only way."

"You knew, didn't you. You knew they were going to take her."

"I may have," she confessed.

"And you pulled me into this anyway?"

"She's our only hope. You were the only person I trusted to protect her. Get her to a safe location then contact me. I will tell you what to do next."

"Dammit!" he exclaimed, rubbing the back of his neck. "This is the last time I help you. Where do you want her?"

Miriam grinned. "Your pick, captain. I've bypassed the jets in the hangar for just long enough not to be detected. Pick any one you want but do it quick before security finds out."

"I hope you know what you're doing, Miriam. This is a mission that will kill us all if it fails."

"I know," she said, and with certainty in her eyes, added, "I trust you'll come through."

Rowen made his way to the hangar. It was a slow day and only a few cargo ships and jets were coming and going. The Ryth soldiers were standing guard at their ship. They didn't turn to see him or acknowledge his presence, but they were aware of his presence. They were a species who took care of business, working diligently, and quickly, but had a natural ability to detect the presence of living things within a hundred feet. What they couldn't do was read minds, so he had to either pretend he was there for something else or explain why he had followed them. Either way, he needed to outsmart them, but first he had to locate the jet he intended to escape in.

One jet caught his eyes—a white fighter jet with a yellow

stripe on the wings. He breathed in deep then walked over nonchalantly toward the Ryths and Aeva.

"Gentlemen," he said. The Ryths turned to him. As expected, they didn't look surprised. "I know you're in a rush to return to *Arcon* with 818 but may I have a word with her before she leaves? It's work related."

"We don't have the time," said Tunjay. Six Ryth guards flanked the *Arcon* chief inspector.

"It won't take long."

Tunjay stared down Rowen. "Five minutes." To the two guards next to him, he said, "Follow them."

Rowen took Aeva's left arm and walked her a few feet away. "There's something on your shoulder," he said and leaned in pretending he was wiping something off her shoulder. While doing so, he whispered in her ear. "We're getting out of here. Follow my lead." Aeva frowned at him. Louder, he cleared his throat and said, "Where did you say you left those files? I didn't find them on my desk."

"Meerton may have taken them off your desk," she played along.

"I'll go see him about it. Thank you."

Aeva turned from him to begin walking back with the guards who were flanking her. When the guards turned to leave, Rowen grabbed a taser blaster from the guard on the right of Aeva and shot him and then shot the other guard. Both guards fell to the ground, unconscious. The guards by the Ryths' ship heard the commotion and made their way toward them. Rowen grabbed Aeva's hand and they ran to the jet.

9

The rain fell heavy and hard, and landing the jet on Stromnair was even harder. There wasn't a runway to descend onto so Rowen maneuvered to an area much like a meadow only it was puddled with water from the constant rainfall and landed with a thud. The last time he was on the planet, he had flown in with a few of his buddies to the main city, Judenome, then rode motorbikes to the wood cabin.

The thud from the landing woke Aeva from sleep. She had dozed off on the flight not being accustomed to space travel. "We've arrived on Stromnair; Merfin Forest, to be exact."

She yawned and looked out the side window observing the rain and the surrounding foliage hidden under an ethereal mist. "It's...beautiful. I've never seen anything like it. It's dreamy."

"You'll have a change of heart after we walk a mile in it to the cabin." He unbuckled his seat belt and helped unbuckle hers.

Stromnair was known as the rain planet for a reason. It

rained a perpetual drizzle for most the year with the exception of three months. The wet and humid environment made it an uncomfortable permanent home. The main town on Stromnair was Judenome with a population just over two thousand. The majority of residences were fish farmers but even they didn't stay year-round. Federation employees who monitored the city worked on rotation, switching out every six months to avoid major depression and migraines.

There were no medications or therapies strong enough to combat the depression. The go-to drug for migraines was Snazatriptan, a green pill the size of a pea. Snaz helped with the migraines caused from the spores in the atmosphere. Natural born humans were susceptible to the migraines, but GENs were not. The Ryths avoided the planet all together. The spores, when in contact with Ryth skin, grew like mold rapidly over their epidermis. The mold would eventually become so thick blanketing every inch of their body, suffocating and killing them. There was no cure. While wearing a secured outfit—similar to a space suit—might promise safety, no Ryths cared to walk around Stromnair in a big, bulky suit.

Rowen looked toward where they would be going but all he saw was haze. "We'll head to the cabin up that hill." He pointed out the front windshield toward barely visible treetops. "There's a path that'll take us directly to it."

By the time they reached the cabin they were soaked through and through. Rowen used his palm to scan his identity and the door opened. They entered the foyer puddling the floor in their wet clothes. "Let's get some dry clothes on then I'll turn on the fireplace and make tea. Sound good?" he said.

"Is this your place?" she asked.

"It belongs to a friend of mine. He gave me access for helping him build it."

They took off their shoes at the entry and walked toward the bedrooms. There were two bedrooms, a master and a smaller room. The smaller room was closer to the entry, so they went in there first to look for clothes. Rowen opened the top dresser. There were nicely folded white t-shirts and sweatpants. "These might be a bit big but they're dry. You probably don't want to be in your jumpsuit anyway," he told her.

"Do you mind if I shower before throwing this on?"

"Not at all. The shower is to the right of the door. There should be towels under the sink."

Rowen had the fireplace going and tea ready when Aeva came out of the shower. He handed her the tea and a hand-size plastic pouch with a spoon in it. "Ration," he said when she gave him a funny look. "It's all we've got in the cabin."

She took the pouch and sniffed the greenish brown mush. It smelled like green bean casserole, which she'd had before, but not in puree style. She took her spoon and stirred the stuff picking up a small portion of the mush and ate it. The flavor was buttery, and to her surprise, tasted like green bean casserole. It was a little on the salty side, but otherwise, it wasn't too bad.

They sat on opposite ends of the couch and ate their rations. The television was on with the Federation news running. Every now and then, Aeva would look up at the news, but for the most part, she ate quietly. Rowen glanced at her as though wanting to say something but didn't. He finished his food with a few big bites then drank his tea. He would contact Miriam later that evening to let her know they were safe and get an update on what to do next. He was sure Miriam would have someone in Judenome who could keep Aeva safe and he could move on.

"Can I have more tea?" Aeva asked when Rowen stood up.

"Sure." He took her cup and went the kitchen. He tossed his empty ration pouch in the recycling machine, then filled her cup with more tea. Afterwards, he searched the cabinets for Snazatriptan. The headache was coming on and would get worse within the next hour. They were deep throbbing pains in the back of his head, pulsing like waves, leaving him immobile.

The amber-colored bottle was in the cabinet above the fridge where his friend kept other medications. He opened the bottle and counted the green pills. Five. He needed one pill a day to remain on the planet. He looked over at Aeva who was eating the last bit of her ration and licking her spoon clean. She would need Snaz too. He'd have to split the pills equally and doing that would only allow them one more day in the cabin. The only way to get more would be to head to the city, to Judenome.

He took a pill with water then went over to her with her tea. He sat the tea down on the coffee table next to her and held out the pill. "Take this."

She looked at the pill in his hand, then at him. "What for?"

"Headaches."

"I don't have a headache."

"You will in about an hour."

"I'll wait."

Stubborn, he thought. He kept the pill in his hand when he took her finished ration packet to the recycling.

"I miss home," she said when he came back and sat next

to her. She was looking out the window at the rain. "I miss my life on *Cana*."

"If I had to work for someone like Tish Carinton, I don't think I'd want to go back."

"She was getting promoted so I wouldn't be seeing her anymore."

"Was that what the meeting was about?" he asked, remembering a day ago when he couldn't get a hold of her at work.

"Pretty much."

"You can't go back to *Cana*."

There was silence and then she wiped tears from her eyes. "It's my home."

"They've brainwashed you," he wanted to say. He wanted to say a whole lot more than that but held his tongue. He needed to contact Miriam to let her know where they were and what the next step was. He too wanted to be somewhere where he could call home. Not here. Not doing someone else's job. It wasn't his responsibility to care for her. Yes, he made the mistake of putting himself in their mess by taking her out of the stranded cargo ship, but he didn't feel he should be responsible for her safety. It was one thing to save someone from dying and another to continue protecting them. The truth would set him free, but it could cause a whole lot of damage to her and Miriam.

What he did say was, "You can't go back any time soon. I'm pretty sure *Arcon* investigators are relentlessly searching for you. We have to lay low for a little while."

She studied him. "Was Miriam right when she said I wouldn't function properly if I left *Cana*?"

"I think so. But you wouldn't just be leaving your environment. They want to do more than interrogate. They—" He paused for a second to phrase his words carefully. "They are speculating that you are part of the rebel regime out to destroy the Federation. They will likely throw out excuses all the while keep you locked in a cell until they get the answers they want from you. Besides that, they'll run tests and probe you, and when they are done testing and probing, they will likely dispose of you."

She frowned. "The chief inspector seemed sincere. He said it over and over that they'd return me."

"They're not going to return you," he stated firmly.

"Does this mean I'll always be running and hiding?"

"No. I'm working with Miriam on what to do next."

"I feel bad that she has to deal with *Arcon* investigators. Do you think she's handling them well?"

Rowen lifted an eyebrow and then turned away from Aeva to hide his surprise. She was a natural just like him, he reminded himself. GENs naturally don't care about others. Off her medications, she was becoming more authentic as a natural human and it made him nervous. "I haven't communicated with her since we left but we'll be in touch in a bit here. You should get to bed. It's getting late."

"Yeah," she said getting up from the couch. He got up too, and for a moment, they stood facing each other in silence. "I might need that green pill. I seem to have this slight throbbing in the back of my head."

Rowen had been holding the pill in his hand and handed it to her. "I had a feeling you'd want it."

That night, after Aeva was in bed in the smaller bedroom, Rowen went to the master bedroom where an emergency communications console was kept hidden in the closet. He turned on the console and a hologram screen opened in front of him. He punched in some code on the keypad and waited. He expected to wait longer but only seconds went by before Miriam's face showed up on the screen. "Teschner, it's a relief to see you. How is 818?"

"She seems to be doing fine. She took a Snaz and went to bed."

"Snaz can make you groggy."

"Tell me about it," he said, sounding more annoyed than sarcastic. Miriam didn't reply but not because of what he'd said. There was a look of nervousness on her face. She kept glancing away from him as though someone else was with her. "Is everything all right?"

She let out a breath. "I'm alone. General Altontaur has sent five shiploads of guards to *Cana*. Two more will come after with replacement personnel. I'm one of the replaced but everything should be set and done before anything drastic happens."

"Why don't you head out here?"

"It's too late. I should have done that when I had the opportunity. They are keeping a close eye on me. I can't talk to you for long, so we have to keep these contacts short."

"What's the plan with Aeva?"

"I have something in mind, but I have to get the security approved first before I can give you more information. I don't want any part of this plan leaked. Once I give you the information, we'll need to move fast."

"How long will it take for approval?"

"It could take up to two weeks."

"Two weeks!" He ran a hand through his hair, frustrated. "We have a problem. We're out in the woods and we're running out of Snaz. There are three pills left between us. I'll need to head to Judenome for more, otherwise we're screwed."

"Judenome is safe. I can get you fake IDs within a couple of days for Snaz."

"We'll leave here tomorrow morning. I'll contact you in Judenome."

"Talk to you soon."

~

ROWEN SWALLOWED his second pill with a glass of water before checking in on Aeva. He had slept in the master bedroom while she slept in the smaller room across from him. He knocked gently on her door. No answer. He reached for the doorknob but stopped before touching it. For a second he had the urge to wake her up but decided to let her sleep. He'd get the motorcycle ready instead.

In the garage was a very expensive onyx supercharged motorcycle and it belonged to his friend. The bike was a beauty, and he was going to ride it to Judenome in the pouring rain—he owed his friend big time. The bike not only goes on the road but it could go above road, hovering a few feet from the ground, a necessity for a rain planet.

When Rowen went back inside the house, a soaked and muddied Aeva stood by the front door shivering and rattled. "What—" he began.

"I came looking for you and slipped on mud. I need another pill."

He grabbed the Snaz from the cupboard. "How long were you standing there?"

"Not long. As soon as I closed the door you came in from the other door."

"The other door is to the garage. I found our ride to Judenome."

Before opening the pill bottle, he grabbed a kitchen towel for her to wipe her face. He wet the towel with a little bit of water from the kitchen sink and handed it to her. She wiped her lips and her cheeks where the mud was still wet. She also wiped her mud-covered hands. While she was wiping down, he opened the bottle and took out a pill. He also filled a glass with water and handed both to her.

"What's Judenome?" she asked before popping the pill in her mouth.

"It's the main city. We need more Snaz. We only have one left. The only place to get more is in the city. You don't want to know what happens if you go 24-hours without Snaz."

"When are we heading out?"

"As soon as you get cleaned up."

10

They arrived in Judenome after a two-hour ride through rolling hills and grassland under a windy and cold rain. The rain was a light mist by the time they reached the city, but still cold, and although it wasn't nighttime, the gray skies made it appear as though it was. High in the sky, a slew of freighter ships flew by, all at different elevations, and all at different levels of loudness. Fishing season had just ended, and these were the last of the freighters taking off with the last catch of the season. Far beyond the hills, lighting flashed, a sign the mist would soon be replaced by hard rain again.

Rowen brought the bike to a stop at the stoplight and looked at the lightning action beyond. The freighters had since passed. with the oncoming rain, it was perfect timing. There were times when the rain got so bad the freighters were forced to land, and in doing so, delayed the fish products being delivered on time. It might not seem like a big deal but large cities like those on Taonos and Pfore depended on these shipments.

The light turned green and he drove down the street

descending slowly down a steep hill where the view of the city lights was barely visible beyond. The rain was coming now, thick and sharp. Rowen knew where he wanted to rent so he picked up speed and headed to the apartment complex.

He rented a furnished studio flat in the complex. He didn't have money on him, but the landlord was willing to trade so he handed over the bike for a month's rent and a cash card enough for at least two-months' worth of food. He was betting on Miriam's plan and wasn't planning on staying longer than two weeks. Whatever he needed was within walking distance, so he didn't miss the bike. His friend would understand. Besides, once he has access to his finances, he'd have the money to repay his friend.

The apartment complex was a ten-story building installed with a voice automated system to control the sound system, television, and outside communications. The studio they rented was one of the smaller units. It was rectangular in shape with the bed in the back where the only window was. The living room separated the kitchen from the bed. The television, embedded in the wall, was across from the couch. It was a quiet and cozy room aside from the sound of the rushing wind and the pounding of rain on the window.

Once they settled in, they headed to a bar called Utiqa for a late lunch. Utiqa not only served liquor, they also served soups and noodle dishes. This place was one of the less busy places to eat and with the fishing done for the season, it was mostly quiet.

Utiqa was next door to the apartment and took but a few steps to reach the entrance. Rowen opened the door for Aeva who was aware of human etiquette from her research into natural human characteristics. It wasn't something

GEN males partook in, mainly because there were no doors to unlatch on the USS *Cana*.

Each ordered a bowl of clam chowder with crackers on the side. When the food arrived and Rowen took a spoonful of clam chowder, it reminded him of the time he was there with Maya. He shouldn't think of her, but he couldn't stop thinking about her. She was perfect in every way. That's how he remembered her anyway. Her soft gray eyes and dark lashes; the way her eyes lit up when she smiled or laughed; the seriousness in her eyes and demeanor when she was getting ready for a mission, and when she was upset; her calmness and understanding. She was smart. How was General Altontaur able to trick her? To blackmail her? Was it possible she liked him?

"Rowen?" Aeva repeated a second time. He finally heard her and turned to her. "Something bothering you?"

"Nothing's bothering me. I was thinking about the last time I was here. What did you ask?"

"I wanted to know if I could have the rest of your crackers."

He pushed his bowl of crackers over to her and while she was putting a few in her chowder, asked, "What were you thinking about?"

"My ex-wife."

"I didn't know you were married. The Federation News never mentioned it."

"We were only married three months before I was forced to annul."

"That's extreme. What happened?"

He thought on it and didn't answer right away. "I guess I don't really know," he finally said. "We got married, I went on a month-long mission, when I returned, I was handed annulment papers and discharged."

"Wow. What did your ex-wife say?"

"Nothing."

"I'm sorry." He didn't say anything, so she continued. "How long did you two know each other before you married?"

"Close to a year."

"That's awhile. I wonder what made her have a change of heart."

Again, he didn't answer her. She returned to her clam chowder and took a few spoonfuls. "At least you can still find someone else to marry," she said after finishing her food.

"It's not that easy to find the right one."

"I don't even have that option—GENs can't marry. Sure sounds romantic though. Living with the one you love for the rest of your life and reproducing."

"You're not missing anything. Besides, right now's not a good time to reproduce."

"Why is that?"

"Breaking up isn't something to be excited about."

"No, I meant the reproducing part."

"It's nothing. We should head back," he said, ignoring her last comment.

"I want to know."

"There's a lot you want to know." He stood up. "We'll talk about it later."

She stared at him for a long time before standing up. Rowen paid for their food and they left.

At the apartment, Aeva didn't let it go. As soon as the door shut behind them, she crossed her arms. "This is later."

Did he really say later? He meant another time far in the future. "It's really not that important—"

She cut him off. "What are you hiding from me?"

"Nothing."

"Because I'm a GEN and too stupid to understand? Is that what you think of me? You think I won't get it."

"Look, if you must know, right now Ryths are taking natural females as Ryth baby incubators. Any naturals able to reproduce will be used for Ryth baby reproduction. There is a shortage of natural females so anyone they think could be a natural will automatically be used for incubating capabilities." There was silence in which Aeva was digesting the information. Rowen continued. "This stuff is irrelevant to you so it's nothing you need to concern yourself over. What's important is that we wait to hear back from Miriam as to what we need to do next to keep you safe."

Aeva looked hard at him. "To keep me *safe*," she repeated. "Safe as in to keep me away from them so that I won't be used as a baby carrier. They tried to kill everyone on the cargo ship to try to find a natural, didn't they?"

Rowen didn't answer her but the look in his eyes said it all.

"I didn't die so they want me because they think I'm a natural. They were never going to interrogate me."

Rowen remained silent.

"That's why I'm here, hiding from them. And, like you said before, they will dispose of me when they find I can't reproduce for them because I'm genetically altered."

"Yes." He swallowed. "But it's not that simple."

"The rebel regime was never a thing."

"It is a thing, but not in your case."

"Don't lie to me. I'm not stupid."

"I—"

"I'm also human, you know," she raised her voice. "Just because I'm not a natural doesn't mean I can't think or feel.

I'm not a heartless creature. I might be genetically made, but I'm still human."

"I'll have to work harder on remembering that."

"You, and naturals like you are so cold-hearted. I don't understand." She went to sit on the couch.

Rowen wanted to explain but he wasn't even sure himself how to explain that he didn't see her as a GEN. He was afraid he might make the mistake of calling her a natural and start a whole new argument with her. This wasn't a good time for that, especially because she's already fired up. He decided to let her cool down. From the looks of it, she didn't seem to want to be bothered. This would be a good time to converse with Miriam on the updates.

"I'm going to see if I can get in touch with Miriam. I'll be back in half an hour."

She ignored him.

THE RAIN WAS a consistent downpour and made it difficult to look up at the neon signs without getting rain on his face and in his eyes. Two blocks away, he saw the one he needed, a blue neon sign that read: *Café Ganolm*.

Inside Café Ganolm, there were two women sitting at a couch sipping their drinks and mingling quietly. In the back, there was a man on a terminal minding his own business. Rowen walked in and sat at a terminal further back. He entered in his passcode and contacted Miriam.

RT: **We're in Judenome.**

. . .

MB: Good to hear from you. How's Aeva?

RT: Slightly upset, but otherwise well.

MB: What upset her?

RT: Something I didn't say.

MB: I see.

RT: How are the ID's coming along?

MB: You should have them by tomorrow morning. I'll be sending the information to the post office. Tell them you're there to pick up an envelope. IDs will be inside. Your ID will allow you to purchase Snazatriptan but not Aeva's. You will have to share the pills, but don't worry. You won't be there long.

RT: What's the status?

MB: You two will be heading to Taonos. I should hear word from entrance security in two days. I will give you the entrance code then. I don't expect any issues with entry. But, Rowen..."

.   .   .

RT: **Yes?**

MB: *Arcon* **military has stepped foot on** *Cana*. **Security is tight. I need to put a little time between our convo to keep them from being suspicious, so contact me in four days. I'll be waiting for you.**

RT: **Will do.**

MB: **Take care of Aeva, will you?**

RT: **Yes.**

MB: **And take care of yourself.**

MIRIAM DISCONNECTED.

11

The next day, Rowen followed Miriam's instructions and went to the post office which was next door to Café Ganolm. Inside, there were no customers and only one mail clerk who was busy arranging boxes from smallest to largest. He looked up upon seeing Rowen and Aeva walking toward the counter. "What can I do for you two?" he asked, eying them closely.

"I have an envelope to pick up," Rowen said.

"Name?"

"Rowen Teschner."

"Teschner?"

"Yes."

The clerk looked from Rowen to Aeva before turning his back to them to dig through the mail. He found the envelope with R. Teschner written on it and handed it to Rowen. "There you go, Mr. Teschner."

They headed to the market three blocks away where Snazatriptan kiosks were. There were ten machines all in a row and looking pristine like they were brand-new. Rowen went to the first machine and inserted his fake ID. He selected the max he was allowed and the machine released it to him. "Let's get lunch by the port. I know a place you'd like," he said, walking away from the machines.

"I need to get some Snaz too," she said.

"Not right now. We have to split what I got."

"That's not going to be enough. Let me get my own." She pulled out her ID and attempted to insert it into the machine.

Rowen stepped in front of her. "We won't need any more than enough for this week. We might only be here for a few days more. If we need more, we'll come back and use your ID. This way they can't track us together."

Aeva put her ID away and they left the store.

Diazog Port was a twenty-minute walk. Rowen regretted selling the motorcycle because it would have taken them five minutes on the bike. He didn't have a choice though. He needed the money. Walking took a little time, but they had nothing else better to do. It was either stay in the apartment watching the news or take a stroll somewhere, and in Judenome, there wasn't much to do. Most people went to the bars lining the main street. Police lingered around some of the busier bars and Rowen preferred not to go anywhere near the police. With his luck he'd get randomly scanned and ID'd and that was the last thing he needed.

The port was closed for the season for commercial fishing; however, Judenome citizens were able to fish throughout the seasons without issue. A few restaurants remained open to cater to visitors and those working seasonal. These restaurants were small eateries owned by the Federation. The cooks and waiters were seasonal employees who were mostly paid volunteers from Taonos and smaller nearby planets and moons.

The restaurant they went to was called Diazog Shack, named after the port. It was a laid-back place resembling a log cabin. The tables and benches were also wood. The waitress who served them was a medical student from Taonos named Zennie Sharpin. She greeted Rowen and Aeva and had two glasses of water ready at their table. "I'm only here three months out of the year," she volunteered the information as the two sat down across from each other. "I prefer the slow season. It allows me to finish my studies on Taonos. I'm a biology major, by the way, going into dentistry. Where are you from?"

"*Cana,*" Aeva said.

"Hey, that's where my study material comes from. I've never been on a ship. How's life there?"

"It's…okay, I guess," Aeva said hesitantly.

Zennie looked at them for a second longer then said, "Let me guess, honeymoon?"

"No—" Aeva began.

"Anniversary," Rowen interjected. "It's our one-year anniversary."

"Oh, that's lovely! Congratulations," Zennie cheered. Her big smile showed perfectly straight and white teeth.

"Thank you," Rowen and Aeva said together.

"I see a lot of couples from *Arcon* but never *Cana*. This is a first for me. What made you decide to celebrate in Judenome?"

"My wife has never seen—"

Before Rowen could finish, the waiter said, "Let me guess, snow."

"Snow?" Aeva said in a bit of surprise.

"Every twenty-five years, snow falls in Judenome," the waiter said. "I guess that's not why you're here," she added, sounding disappointed.

"You're right. I've heard about that. When will it happen? We might want to stay for it," Rowen said, glancing at Aeva.

"Should be within the next few days."

"Well then, we'll definitely be here for it," he said, but he wasn't so sure.

Aeva agreed and nodded.

"This will be my first time too and I don't plan to miss it. Now, what would the two of you like to order?"

Zennie took their order and left. When she was out of view, Aeva glared at Rowen. "One-year anniversary. Couldn't you have said we're friends?"

"Saying anything else and she'll be asking us questions right and left. It's simpler to say we're married." Just as Rowen finished talking, the screen on the wall rolling the daily news showed a picture of him and Aeva.

"...these two fugitives have not been found yet," the reporter said. "As a reminder, one is a natural and a former captain of the Absolution Rescue Mission Team who goes by the name of Rowen Teschner. The other one is a female GEN named Aeva 818. General Krane Altontaur of the USS *Arcon* and Chief Inspector Tunjay Tharunbat are asking for your help in turning these two over to authorities. They are armed and extremely dangerous."

"Armed and extremely dangerous? That's not true," Aeva said, frowning.

"It doesn't matter. Looks like it's repeated news. It must have aired as soon as we left *Cana*. We'll need to lie low."

"What if someone already saw us and reported it. What if the waiter..." Aeva covered her mouth with both hands; her eyes frantically staring at the kitchen door the waiter went through.

"She didn't seem very suspicious. She believed we were married. Besides, we just got here yesterday. I don't think anyone expected us here this quickly and I doubt they've put our faces to the photos. We'll need to disguise ourselves though until I hear back from Miriam. I'll drop by the store after we eat to get hair dye and a wig for you."

"That guy at the post office looked at us weird."

"I noticed that too. The thing is, Judenome is a sanctuary planet for fugitives so even if he recognized us, he might not report us. This is the safest place for us."

Zennie returned with their meals a few minutes later. The waitress had a big beautiful smile and bright eyes and seemed to have been clueless as to the news. If she had seen the news before, she didn't show any signs that it was of any importance to her. "Enjoy!" she exclaimed and left.

Neither were very hungry after seeing the news but ate what they could stomach. Zennie returned shortly and presented them with a cake with the words, *Happy 1ˢᵗ Anniversary* written in icing. "Complimentary," she said, grinning. "You two look a little gloomy. I hope this will cheer you up."

They thanked her and ate what they could of the cake taking home the rest. They also took the rest of their meals to go. Rowen paid, tipping Zennie generously.

12

The new look wasn't so bad for Rowen. He'd decided to bleach his black hair a dirty blond. Just that small change made him look like a whole new person. Aeva wore a natural-looking, auburn-colored wig that fell just below her shoulders. Rowen found it difficult to look away from her because she too appeared to be a whole new person. He preferred her natural light-brown hair; it accentuated her chestnut-colored eyes nicely, but this wasn't his choice. Besides, it was only a wig.

They were at Utiqa for breakfast three days later and the news about *Arcon* taking over *Cana* came on the monitors. Briefly, the reporter stated that there were not enough humans to man the sister ship so *Arcon* had no choice but to step in, adding that it was their responsibility to care for *Cana* and the humans on board. Rowen knew it was propaganda to make *Arcon* look good. That pissed him off so much so that he wanted to throw his coffee at the monitor, but that wouldn't fix anything. Instead, he turned from the monitor and ignored the rest of the news. He thought about Miriam. Would she now be working for *Arcon* Ryths or would she be removed from her position? Was this what she meant by 'tighter security'? It worried him, but he had faith in her. She had always come through, even when situations were at their worst.

"Does this mean I'll never be able to return to *Cana* after all this stuff with C24 settles?" Aeva asked, eyes glued to the monitor.

"Might not be wise," he answered without looking at her.

Their breakfast came. Each had ordered omelets with a side of pancakes and coffee as their choice of drinks. They ate without talking. Aeva would look up every now and then at the news while he continued to ignore it.

After they finished, the bartender, who was wiping the counter said, "Looks like it's going to happen soon." He nodded his head at them to look out the large windows. There were people going outside and standing around looking up at the sky.

"The snow," Aeva whispered. "Let's go see it." She grabbed his right hand, intertwining her fingers with his as they made their way out the door.

They stood among the people who were also waiting for the snow. Some were chatting with those they stood next to and others stood alone. The rain earlier had come to a complete stop during the time they were inside the bar. Now, it was only the cold they had to deal with.

They had released hands and Rowen tucked his in his jacket to keep warm. Aeva had her arms wrapped around her chest. They both glanced up at the sky which was a lighter gray now than it was earlier. "Maybe we should wait inside," Rowen said noticing Aeva shivering.

She didn't reply and only looked at him with dreamy eyes. She moved a little closer to him and cupped his jaw closer to her face. Before he could say or do anything—and maybe he wanted it too, she slowly and gently kissed him on the lips. A part of him wanted to push her away. Not because he didn't want to kiss her, but because it was wrong. All wrong. But he didn't. He didn't resist even though he knew he should. His hands had a mind of their own and went to her waist, pulling her closer to him, closing the gap between them.

Her lips were soft and warm, and he wanted more of it. When she opened her mouth slightly, he wasted no time diving in with his tongue. Their tongues danced together in the warmth of each other's mouth and the world disappeared around them.

The air had gotten colder, but it didn't matter to him because the warmth from their kiss radiated throughout his body, tingling every inch of him, burning the deepest part of him, setting his soul on fire. He couldn't remember the last time he felt this much desire.

His conscience stepped in after a minute or so and he pulled her away. "We can't," he whispered, catching his breath.

She was breathing hard too. Her lips were pink, her cheeks were flushed, and she was irresistible. She bit down on her lower lip which made him want to pull her close again and kiss those lips, but he had to contain himself.

"What was that for?" she asked, touching her lips. To her, the kiss felt like it was the last kiss, a good-bye kiss, as though they were lovers and were never going to see each other again.

"I...I didn't mean to," was all he managed.

Aeva didn't say anything else, but the look on her face made him feel guilty. He was preparing for the worst while she wanted to live in the moment. Why was he so cautious?

What did it matter? He knew, but a part of him denied it. He's reminded himself a thousand times, it seems, that she was to be protected. Things would be different if he didn't have to worry about that.

She stepped away from him and as she did, a snowflake landed on her cheek and then another a few seconds after. She looked up at the sky, squinting and blinking a few times to keep the snowflakes from dancing into her eyes. "It's snowing," she said and held her palm out to catch the tiny soft ice crystals that melted on contact with her skin. She stretched out her arms and closed her eyes and let the tiny flakes dance onto her face. She began to slowly turn—arms still outstretched, and mouth opened to taste the fragile snowflakes on her tongue.

Rowen watched her in amusement, captivated by her tendency to get lost in the moment, by how she lived in the here and now, and how she was able to enjoy the little things while they were in a dire situation. In that moment he knew something was different about his feelings for her. It was a warm and intense yearning deep within, sparking an urge to protect her, not because Miriam said to, but because he wanted to. It occurred to him that if he were to lose her somehow, whether by his own lack of safeguarding her or by the natural progression of fate, he would be crushed.

The snow only lasted a few minutes before the rain began to fall again. Rowen had planned to make a stop at Café Ganolm to contact Miriam. When they arrived at the coffeehouse, it was busy, and all the terminals were occupied. The wait would be at least one hour, two. Instead of waiting around, they grabbed coffee and returned to the apartment. He'd come back later.

That evening, they had leftover noodles from Utiqa for

dinner and took their Snaz with water. The news was on, covering everything from thieves to rebels to new technology and military defense.

During a commercial, Aeva said, "Rowen, when you said it wouldn't be wise to return to *Cana*, it made me wonder where I'd end up. I always thought I would live my life on *Cana*. It never crossed my mind that I'd live anywhere else. It scares me to think I could never return there. I'm also worried about my well-being. What will happen to me if I'm out of my environment longer than I should be?"

"You'll return eventually, just not anytime soon. I don't have a timeframe to give you."

"If I have to go anywhere other than *Cana*, I think I'd like to go with you. The universe is so big I can't imagine getting around alone. You seem to know what you're doing and where you're going."

"You don't want to go where I go," he asserted.

She thought on his words. "Do you think there's a chance things will fall through and I'll end up on *Arcon*?"

"I've worked with Miriam in the past. She never fails."

They finished eating and while he was throwing their empty noodle cartons in the trash and putting their cups in the dishwasher, she was watching the news. The reporter mentioned the Century Ball and he saw the look of disappointment on her face. He felt guilty at not coming through with his promise to her. Lately, that's been his thing.

She spoke to the voice automated system to shut off the television monitor then took a deep breath before standing up. "I'm going to bed."

He went over to her. "I'm sorry about the Ball."

"At least we saw snow, right?" She looked at him, trying to stay positive.

"Will you dance with me?" It came out of him unexpectedly, but it was too late to turn back now.

She stood there speechless; mouth half opened. He took her hands in his and began to sway in the silence. To the voice automated system, he asked it to play a slow song. The music began, opening with mellow drums leading into a soulful mid-tempo doo-wop similar to the classics of the 1950's and 60's from Earth. A woman's voice began singing in a high and soft, sweet voice.

He pulled her close wrapping both his hands around her waist. She ran her hands over his chest and rested them on his shoulders as they rhythmically moved to the music. He looked into her eyes. This close to her he could see the sprinkle of freckles across her nose. And those lips. They were plump and so soft looking he wanted to put his own lips on them. He tingled all over thinking about it and felt his manhood harden.

He leaned in to kiss her and she kissed back. He moved his tongue inside her mouth. She tasted sweet and it was intoxicating. He kissed her harder and she didn't back away. His heart was pounding, and he was sure she could hear it, but he didn't care. He was yearning to be with this woman, to feel every inch of her body, to be deep inside her.

He carried her to the bedroom and undressed her before taking off his own clothes. He ran his fingers over her jawline toward her chin and leaned in for a deep kiss. While his mouth was on hers, his hands went down her back to her buttocks and he cupped them, squeezing gently. She was breathing deep and a moan escaped her lips. It made his manhood even harder.

She got on the bed and he went on top of her, kissing her stomach, moving up to her round and soft breasts, suckling one while caressing the other. He gently separated her legs and positioned himself between them. When he touched her womanly spot with his fingers, she arched her back and let out a breathy moan. He slipped two fingers inside her. She was wet and ready for him. He moved his shaft between her slit and slowly penetrated. The first few thrusts were gentle and then he pushed all the way inside, filling every inch of her. She took in a quick breath and gripped his arms as his manhood expanded her. She let out a soft moan that became louder as he rocked her. The sound of her voice excited him, and he rocked harder and harder, thrusting in and out. They moved together in rhythm, mixing sweat, kissing. He wanted to go slower to make it last longer, but his manhood refused to hold back. He was ready to cum. He lifted her legs up over his shoulders then pumped her with a few quick thrusts, with the final one delving deep inside her, releasing his seeds into the depths of her womanhood. They climaxed together with her crying out in ecstasy. Her legs trembled under him and he knew she was satisfied just as he was.

13

After their lovemaking, Aeva fell asleep. Rowen was wide awake and watched the rain drizzle down the windowpane. He followed each vein-like streak wiggle its way down. While his eyes were on the rain, his mind drifted to Aeva. They had made love only a few hours earlier. His manhood was throbbing for her again, but his mind felt guilty, or was it his heart that was heavy with guilt? He never meant to kiss her, to touch her soft and shapely body, to make love to her. It wasn't supposed to happen. He was supposed to keep her safe not make love to her. Maybe it wasn't guilt but shame that he went against Miriam's wishes to protect her. But he was protecting her, wasn't he? And he didn't use her to relieve himself, he knew that for sure. He's been with very attractive women, but he never needed or wanted to sleep with them. Yet, he made love to Aeva. He eventually drifted to sleep with guilt on his mind.

A loud thunder woke him up. The alarm clock on the bedside table read 4:30 a.m.

"Rowen?" Aeva was awake too.

"Yeah?"

"Was that thunder?"

"Yeah."

"It scares me."

"It's normal. Go back to sleep."

"I can't. I'm awake now."

A bright flash of light flew across the sky and lit the room for a few second. Thunder followed loud enough that Aeva covered her ears. Rowen pulled her close to him and kissed her. They made love again. Afterward, Rowen got up and showered. He dressed and went to brew coffee. He opened the cupboard and reached for the coffee bag. There was enough for one cup. He'd meant to grab some earlier but forgot.

"I'm heading out to get us more coffee and breakfast at Café Ganolm. I'm also going to contact Miriam while I'm there. You want to come?"

Aeva sat up and rubbed her eyes. "You go ahead. I need to shower anyway."

"Okay. Be back soon."

Café Ganolm was empty except for the barista who was busy stocking coffee cups. Rowen went to the back and sat at a terminal. He logged in using the name on his fake ID. He didn't want to take chances with his real name after learning that *Arcon* had invaded *Cana*.

Once logged in, he contacted Miriam.

The message on the screen read: **Access Denied.**

Maybe he typed her name wrong. His fingers were cold. He rubbed his fingers in his palms to warm them up and tried again.

Access Denied.

Confused, he tried one more time, typing slower.

Access Denied.

He decided to do a search on her in the public database for a status on her record. The word *DECEASED* in red blinked next to her photo. "Shit!" he shouted.

The barista looked over at him. "You all right?"

"Sorry, it's all good," he replied.

A police officer walked in at that moment and made eye contact with him. His heart began to race. They've caught us, he thought. He knew it would happen. Stay calm, he told himself. Stay calm and do as the officer says.

The officer quickly diverted his attention to the barista and ordered his drink. Rowen let out a breath of relief.

Miriam was dead. What now? How was he to get the code to Taonos? Who on *Cana* could get into Miriam's files and send it to him? What about the placement resource personnel, Liz? She was nice to him—impatient, but nice. Truthfully, he couldn't trust her with the current situation. Damn. Where were the people he trusted when he needed them most? They seemed to disappear at the most disadvantageous time.

He sat at the terminal for a while longer thinking about what to do. It was up to him now to decide Aeva's fate.

An hour later, he returned to the apartment with the coffee and breakfast sandwiches. He knocked on the door. Aeva opened it and saw the look of dismay on his face. "You're a bit gloomy, something happened?"

He put the groceries on the counter and opened the coffee bag to begin making the coffee. "I didn't get the entry code."

"What did Miriam say? Maybe it's just a delay."

He wasn't going to tell her that Miriam was dead. She might panic. He needed time to plan. Alone. But, when he looked at Aeva, at her eyes, there was a sadness, a guilty kind of sadness that washed over him. He'd been lying to her all this time. He went back and forth between telling her the truth and not telling her the truth. The truth would set him free, but it would put all the burden on her. Did he really want that? At first, she might be upset at him for lying but eventually she'd forget about him. But then, she'd have to deal with whatever was to come with the Ryths. She'd have to surrender her body to them. And then, surrender the chip, which equated to destroying humankind, and he didn't want to go down in history as the person who caused the extinction of humans.

"Yeah, she said check back with her tomorrow," he lied.

Aeva frowned. "You don't sound so sure."

Rowen took a deep breath. "There was a police officer who walked into the café. I thought they'd found us, but he was only there for coffee. It got me worried, that's all."

"It sounds like we're not safe here anymore."

"We are safe. It's been more difficult to get in touch with Miriam now because Ryths have infiltrated *Cana* and have taken over the ship. Miriam wouldn't give them our location but there is a possibility they could force it out of her."

"Don't you find it a little absurd what Ryths are doing? They are taking over *Cana* and forcing Miriam to tell them where I'm at just because they think I could be a natural. It just doesn't make sense. They know I'm genetically engineered. They have my birth information. What do they still want with me?"

Rown swallowed. "You have a valid point."

She went and kissed him on the lips. It was a long kiss, just her lips on his. When she stepped back, she asked, "What did you get for breakfast?"

"Sausage and egg sandwiches."

Rowen was quieter than normal and barely touched his food which prompted Aeva to say, "Rowen, sometimes I can't read you. It's like I think I know you and then the next thing, you make me feel like I'm this crazy GEN who's going out of control. We make love and I think you must really like me, but here you are, distancing yourself and being secretive." She looked to the floor then back at him. "If I did anything wrong, let me know. I can work on it. GENs are not perfect."

A slight grin fell on his lips. He'd forgotten she thought of herself as a GEN. Would she believe she was a natural if she were told she was?

"Okay," he said. "There's nothing you need to worry about. I won't let you get into the wrong hands. I promise. We'll get through this."

"I trust you."

FOR THE NEXT couple of days, every time Rowen went out alone, he'd make excuses. Sometimes it was to get in touch with Miriam or to grab something from the café or Utiqa Bar. Truth was he needed more time to plan. He was getting depressed and it wasn't only because of Miriam's death. The spores were beginning to affect him. The sun, surprisingly, made a visit the day before. It was visible for no more than an hour, and even though it warmed the city, it wasn't enough to cure his impending depression.

A week and half later, Rowen sluggishly threw on his jacket. "I'm going to contact Miriam. She said today was the day. I'll get lunch for us too. Anything in particular you like?"

"A turkey sandwich sounds good."

"Turkey sandwich it is."

He crossed the street to Café Ganolm. At the terminal,

he didn't bother trying to connect to Miriam. He was sure her office and computer were confiscated and searched for information on Aeva's whereabouts. Instead, he searched her profile in the deceased database looking for cause of death. What came back was: *unknown.* Unknown could mean a number of things. It could mean they are examining the cause of death and are awaiting results. It could mean they don't have anyone on *Cana* yet who can do the exam and she's being held in a freezer. It could also mean they don't know. Usually, if they don't know, an examiner would put a note in her file stating unknown cause, but that too can take time because the examiner would need time to fill out all kinds of paperwork and then log the information in her file.

Fifteen minutes later, he logged off the terminal. Miriam was gone and that left him in charge of Aeva. He could decide whatever he wanted with Aeva. Taonos was not a choice anymore. Without the entry code, he couldn't enter the planet's atmosphere. They'd take him in as a prisoner if he tried.

He had two choices. Stay on Stromnair a little longer but get out of Judemone and find a place in another city to hide in. It would mean putting up with depression and stealing Snaz. This would buy time for him to plan an escape. He'd be able to locate the exoplanets. The other choice was to turn himself and Aeva in. He could argue that he decided it was the right thing to do. This might still get him locked up, but it'd only be for six months to a year. It could even be less. He'd move on with his life and Aeva...well, he'd forget about her by then.

He stayed at the terminal for ten more minutes. Any longer and Aeva would go looking for him. He stood up, stretched, yawned, then walked out of Café Ganolm.

14

R owen knocked on the door.

"Who is it?" Aeva said from the other side.

"It's me."

She unlocked the door and swung it open. "I'm starving. You got the—" She didn't finish her words because flanking Rowen were two police officers.

"I'm sorry," he said, and for a brief second his eyes locked on hers, but the guilt was too heavy on him and he couldn't bring himself to look at her again.

"Rowen?" She took a step back from the door. "What's going on?" She looked to the officers then back to him. Her eyes drifted to his left arm where one of the officers had a grip. Then, it occurred to her that he was handcuffed seeing how both his hands were behind his back. "What did you do?" She took a few more steps away from the door.

One of the officers stepped in front of Rowen. "Are you 818?" the officer asked.

"Yes."

"You're under arrest for violating the statutes of the Federation. You'll be escorted to *Arcon* immediately."

"Wait—" She looked to Rowen. "Tell me what's going on first?" She pleaded, searching his face for answers, but he gave nothing away. "Rowen, you didn't."

"I had to."

"You said we were safe."

"I'm sorry, Aeva."

The officer who had stepped inside was now cuffing her hands. "Take me to *Cana*," she demanded. "That's where I'm from. Miriam will explain everything."

"Orders are to *Arcon*," the officer said.

She turned to Rowen. "You said I'd be safe." He didn't say anything. "You're a fucking liar. I hope I never see you again."

"We're going to the same place," he said, but she only glared at him.

THE JET RIDE went through hyperspace and arrived at the USS *Arcon* within two hours. Rowen wasn't surprised to find the mothership docked at the Ryths' space station. General Altontaur wasted no time, as usual.

The officers flanked him and Aeva toward the security room. From there, the officers handed them to *Arcon* guards. The guards walked them down a corridor and turned a few more corners before they reached the investigation room.

Tunjay Tharunbat stood by the door awaiting them. A pleasing grin was on his lips as though he'd been waiting for this moment. "Being on the run isn't as fun as you'd thought, now is it," Tunjay said as they were shuffled into the room.

Rowen said nothing.

"It wasn't my idea." Aeva scowled at Rowen.

"Well, I'm glad you're here," the chief inspector said, pleased.

"I'm glad to be here," Aeva said to spite Rowen. He didn't show any emotions, whatsoever.

Tunjay tapped his fingers together. "General Krane Altonataur will be here shortly. In the meantime, make yourselves comfortable."

When the general entered the room, heads turned. There was an aura about the Ryth leader. His physical presence pervaded every room he walked into. This day was no different. Tall and lean, he was built like a warrior. His chiseled jaw, deep-set eyes, and heavyset eyebrows gave him a deceiving appearance. He was handsome in a pleasant kind of way.

Tunjay waited until the general stood in front of Rowen and Aeva before speaking. "General, your guests." His grin earlier was now a big smile spreading across his face.

The general took a step closer to Aeva. "Aeva, is it?"

"Yes," she answered.

"You're very pretty, Aeva. Had I known you were stranded on Stromnair I would have sent someone to extract you from that despicable place. I hear it's depressing there. I apologize for not thinking more of your safety."

"I was safe."

"Teschner would make you believe so. Do you know why he turned you over?" He spoke as if Rowen wasn't in the room.

She didn't know because he'd refused to tell her when she'd asked. Still, her indignation didn't give him away.

The general took a step even closer until he was only inches from her face. "Nevermind that. While you were there, did you take the green pill, Snazooo—"

Aeva took a step back. "Snazatriptan. All humans have to take it."

"All humans? Including the lesser kind, the genetically mutated?"

She frowned at him. "Yes."

"You had the headaches?"

"Ryths wouldn't know, now would you?"

The general grinned. "Teschner didn't tell you the truth, did he?"

"What do you mean?"

Altontaur laughed. "Your friend is a fool—"

"He's not my friend. He was doing his job."

"Oh? Yes, that's right. He was volunteering for Chief Investigator Miriam Butterford. How could I have overlooked Butterford. She was trying to protect you with his help. A stupid decision on her part, if you ask me. It's unfortunate she's dead."

Aeva gasped. "No! she's not—"

Altontaur cut her off. "Teschner didn't tell you that either? I'm assuming he turned you over because she's no longer with us. She was the one protecting you. When she died, there was no one else. Teschner wasn't going to do the job, as proven with your presence here. He was either paid or he owed Miriam something. You see, Teschner was expelled from *Arcon*. He can't step foot on this ship. Doing so would mean death. This is why I don't understand why he would send you here. He must know what you really are."

Aeva looked at Rowen. "And what's that?"

The general continued. "Let's start from the beginning, shall we? You see, you survived the cargo hijack because you're immune to the chemical that was released. It was meant to kill GENs. There was another chemical in the cockpit which killed the two natural pilots. You were lucky enough to get the end of that otherwise you would be dead too, which wouldn't be an issue really.

"Now, as for the green pill, I wasn't aware that you weren't aware GENs were immune to the headaches. Only natural humans have to take the pill. GENs are mutated to withstand the spores causing the headaches. In other words, my dear, you are not a GEN."

The news befuddled Aeva and she had difficulty digesting it. She wanted to say something, but nothing came out.

"We could have avoided the interrogation altogether and bring you directly here, but Miriam wouldn't allow it. She made it difficult for all of us."

"So you killed her."

"Her demise was her own doing. It's not in our nature to kill."

"You infiltrate *Cana* in which Miriam mysteriously dies all because she didn't want me to incubate your Ryth babies?"

The general raised his eyebrows. "*Cana* is the sister-ship. When I became general, I owned *Cana*. Admiral Johnston was...you say could say, my puppet. I could have sent Ryths over much earlier, but I chose not to because I care about humans. We had no choice when Miriam chose to go against us. She was unwilling to help us determine why you survived the cargo incident. As far as incubating Ryth babies go, I would never force naturals to do such a thing. Only those who want to help willingly will do so."

"What is it that you want from me?"

The general looked at her for a long time before saying, "A crime was committed on that cargo ship and then you decide not to cooperate. What do you think?"

"Tell her the truth," Rowen interrupted. "Tell her what your ultimate goal is."

The general's attention turned to Rowen. "I almost forgot you existed. You never seem to completely go away."

"You stole Captain Teschner's wife," Aeva interrupted, bringing the general back to her.

"Maya Seymour? She made her own decision to be with me. I did nothing to persuade her."

That son-of-a-bitch. Rowen wanted to put a fist in Altontaur's face for lying. His ex-wife was blackmailed. A part of him was glad Aeva challenged him but another part of him wished she hadn't gone there. He regretted telling her about his marriage, but there was nothing he could do now.

"Rowen said—"

"Rowen would make you believe I'm the enemy. He's a pathetic man with nothing to him. If his ex-wife really loved him, she wouldn't have left him. It sounds like he tried to brainwash you before bringing you to me. I hope you learn to use your own *natural* brain, Aeva. You sound intelligent. Now, let's not talk about my wife anymore. It is you I'm interested in."

"I can't imagine you'd want anything else from me if not my uterus."

"I don't want you for your uterus. There's more to you than you know, but let's get you scanned and evaluated, all of which are normal procedures, and then we'll talk." He turned to the chief inspector. "Tunjay, will you walk Aeva over to Medical. There are a few things Teschner and I need to talk about."

"At your command, general." Tunjay went over to stand next to Aeva. She looked at Altontaur as though she had something else to say to him but then turned to follow Tunjay.

"I have nothing to say to you," Rowen said after the door closed behind Aeva and Tunjay.

The general stared at him with disgust. "Take him to the brig." A guard nearby stepped forward. "I'll deal with him later. I have business to take care of at the moment."

The guard walked Rowen to the brig in the lower deck. When they were down the corridor near the brig where no one else was around, Rowen punched the guard in the stomach and then an uppercut, knocking the Ryth out cold. He switched into the guard's uniform before dragging the guard into a cell and hitting the on-button for the forcefield bars.

The USS *Arcon* was a massive ship and with having lost half of its human workers within the last two decades due to the Khardavirus, it never caught back up to its full crew capacity. With General Altontaur in position, he was staffing the crew with Ryths, but due to strict rules by the Federation, it took months for background checks to complete, and thus left sections of the ship unattended.

Luck was on Rowen's side when he went down the corridors of *Arcon*. There was not a guard in sight. He made his way to Medical and walked in. At the front desk was a Ryth receptionist. "Can I help you?" she asked.

"I'm looking for patient 818."

"Let me look them up." The receptionist went to her desk, set her coffee down, and clicked a few buttons on her screen. "You said, 818?"

"818."

"Doesn't look like we have an 818."

"Can you look her up by name? Aeva, A-E-V-A."

The receptionist typed in the name. "There is an Aeva."

"What room?"

"She's not here."

"Where is she?"

"I can't disclose that, sir."

He pulled out his laser gun and she gasped when he pointed it at her. "Tell me."

"I-I'm not authorized to share personal information."

"Tell me. Now."

"Captain Teschner, what are you doing here?" said a voice from Rowen's left. He turned the laser gun toward the voice. It was the ship's physician, Dr. Ariny DeShevell.

"Where's Aeva?" Rowen said, blaster at the doctor's head.

Dr. DeShevell didn't look frightened at all at seeing the weapon pointed at her. In fact, she was too calm, and it made Rowen nervous. "Why don't we talk."

"Just tell me where she is."

"She's in her cabin, resting. I need to talk to you so why don't we go to my office."

Rowen put the laser gun away and followed the doctor into her office. She sat at her desk and gestured for Rowen to sit in the seat across from her. He chose to stand. "How do I stop Altontaur from fucking her."

The doctor was taken aback. "What are you talking about?"

"You know what I'm talking about." He tried to hold back his anger, but he was losing his patience. He was tired of all the mind games from the Ryths. "Damn it! Tell me how I can stop the general from taking another natural."

"I don't understand, captain."

"I've lost someone once to him. It's not going to happen again."

"Are you saying General Altontaur has plans to harm Aeva?"

"You don't know his plans? Tell me you're kidding."

"There's a misunderstanding. Aeva was brought here to be scanned for an object that was to be removed from her back."

"I know that. It's a chip with data."

"Correct, but there's more. Before scanning, I did a full examination. It's concluded that she is a natural. She is also pregnant."

It took a second for Rowen to register what Dr. DeShevell had said. The news made him stumble backwards against the wall. "What? I—I—"

"You might want to take a seat to hear the rest, captain." Rowen wasted no time sitting down. "The blood work came back positive that you are the father. Your DNA is on file and it matched."

He blushed. "I thought she was provided with birth control. Wait, she wouldn't have needed it because she lived among GENs and male GENs can't reproduce. I overlooked her reproductive possibility." He said the last few words mainly to himself.

"Her file says she was on birth control, but she was taken off all medications at one point, including the birth control. It would seem odd that a GEN would need birth control but there have been cases where a genetically created human is born with that defect. In those cases, they are given the birth control. She was a defect; therefore, she was on birth control.

"In cases where a defect gets pregnant, an abortion would be done. Since Aeva is a natural, it isn't required that she has an abortion. However, because of her situation, an abortion will eliminate any unnecessary uncertainty."

"I don't want her to abort."

"I wasn't asking."

Rowen opened his mouth to say something, but the doctor continued. "By the way, I thought you were exiled. I'm guessing the general doesn't know you're here, Officer Baldor." She eyed the guard uniform Rowen was wearing. Her eyes landed on his left shoulder where the name, Freddie Baldor was stitched to his shirt.

"I'd like it that way. How far along is she?"

"About a week along. The general wants the abortion and the chip removed at the same time."

"It's against Federation law to abort a natural fertilization after 72 hours."

"That's correct. However, Ryth laws has jurisdiction in Ryth territory, and this is Ryth territory."

"Fuck your Ryth laws," he scowled. "Fuck all of this!" He stood up, grabbed his chair and slammed it against the wall behind him. "That bastard! I'll kill him!" he exclaimed, kicking and punching the wall.

The doctor stood up. "Calm down, captain. If you don't calm down, I will have to call the guards."

"Do you realize Aeva is carrying my child? My flesh and blood!"

"I do, but there's nothing I can do."

"The general wants to kill my baby so that he can use Aeva to carry his Ryth babies. Do you not understand that?" Rowen ran his hands through his hair. Sweat was beading at his temples from his rage.

There was finally calm after another bout of wall punching. In that moment of stillness, he looked at the doctor and saw that she was frightened. "I'm sorry. I didn't mean to react like that. It's because..." he took a deep breath in and a deep breath out. "We're being wiped out—my kind is being wiped out. I know Ryths are also fighting a lost battle but it's not right to take human females as incubating substitutes. Their bodies are not meant for that. There has to be a better solution."

"I understand, captain, and I apologize for what we've done to naturals. I agree there are better solutions. We should work together to find a cure, not destroy another race such as your own. I didn't realize Aeva was a natural. Now I understand why you're angry with General Altontaur. If there's anything you need me to do, I'll do my best."

Rowen raised an eyebrow. "There is something."

"What is it?"

"The chip in Aeva contains important data. If you can get that chip to me, I'd appreciate it."

Dr. DeShevell thought on it. "I can try," she said.

Rowen rubbed his neck. "Does Aeva know she's pregnant?"

"She doesn't know. As I said earlier, the general's plan was to abort during the chip removal. She'd never guess she was ever pregnant."

"Will you promise you won't abort the baby?"

Dr. DeShevell nodded.

"When will you do the chip removal?"

"Tomorrow morning at 5 a.m."

"How will you get the chip to me?"

"Come by after the surgery and I'll give it to you."

"How do I know you won't abort the baby?"

"You'll have to trust me, captain."

Rowen went looking for the escape pods after leaving Medical. He remembered seeing the pods before but didn't think much of them assuming they were regular escape pods. Now he realized they were unique.

As he walked down the hall toward the pods, a man's voice yelled, "Stop right there or we'll shoot!"

Rowen stopped in his track. He recognized the voice. It was the security officer he had given the chokehold to. He didn't think the guy would track him down, but who was he kidding? Ryths revel in a good revenge.

"Put your gun down and slowly turn around," one of the other officers said. Rowen did as he was asked.

"It's him and he's in my uniform," the officer named Freddie Baldor said. Both officers had their photon blasters pointed at Rowen.

From behind the two officers, stepped forward Tunjay with a sly grin on his lips. "Being sneaky won't help you," he said to Rowen. "Bring him."

They brought Rowen to the brig, and as they were about

to put him in a holding cell, Officer Baldor kneed him in the groin. Rowen grunted bending forward from the excruciating pain.

Baldor laughed in vindictive delight. "You piece of shit," he muttered and elbowed Rowen in the left jaw.

The force from the elbow threw Rowen in a half spin toward the floor. His hands caught his fall stopping his head from slamming onto the ground. Baldor kicked him a few times on the side and he groaned in pain. Fighting back was tempting. It would be easy. All he had to do was swing his left leg at Baldor's ankle and the Ryth would fall hard on his ass; He'd grab for the gun on the Ryth's belt and shoot all four Ryths, ending the whole thing within seconds, but doing so would be counterproductive to his goal of getting Aeva into a pod. He would only make it worse for himself because even if he was successful in the brig, the security camera would capture it all and a squad of officers would arrive in seconds.

"Enough!" Tunjay exclaimed. "Put him in the holding cell. Now!" The officers picked Rowen up and threw him in the cell and turned on the force field. "You two keep watch," he told two of the officers. "Baldor, you come with me. I will not have you kill Teschner before General Altontaur has his moment with him."

Rowen pushed himself against the wall and sat up. He grunted and coughed and wrapped his arms around his middle section where the pain was still throbbing. Breathing hurt but he forced himself to take in big gulps of air. Baldor did a number on him and now he wished he'd fought back.

A few hours passed and he was feeling better when he heard shuffling feet and voices coming toward his cell. It was none other than General Krane Altontaur, and with him was Aeva. They were dressed in elegant clothing as though attending a party.

"Why am I not surprised?" Altontaur said, looking at Rowen with abhorrence.

"Rowen?" Aeva said, standing inches from the force field door. A perplexed expression crossed her face as she noted his blood crusted lips and bruises on his face. Her voice had a genuine concern to it, and it put a slight smile on the corner of his lips. But all too quickly, she squinted with the coldest stare he'd ever seen from her. She turned to the general. "What's he doing here?"

"You tell me," the general said.

"I thought you put him in a cabin."

"He was found snooping around. You have any knowledge as to why?"

"He turned me in. You think I would know?" To Rowen she said, "General Altontaur told me everything you refused to tell me."

"Aeva." Rowen sounded disappointed. "He's a liar. Don't believe anything he says." He stood up and walked near the force field to get a better look at her. She had not been claimed yet and was relieved.

"I'm the daughter of the late General Thomas Cloudon. My father ran this ship. My grandfather ran this ship and great grandfather ran the first fleet out here. You knew all this and you kept it from me."

"It wasn't important at the time. I was going to tell you someday."

"I have access to earth," she added.

"I know."

"Were you going to tell me that someday too?"

Rowen glanced at the general who looked satisfied. "Yes."

"I don't know who you are anymore. I can't trust you."

"Did the general tell you you're pregnant with our baby?" His words surprised her and she didn't know what to say. "Come on, Altontaur. I thought you could do better," Rowen said to the general.

Altontaur clenched his jaw and swallowed before he spoke. "You *are* with child," he confessed to Aeva. "You'll be in good care. That is nothing for you to be concerned about. Now is not the time to talk about something as precious as your baby—not to mention your health and overall well-being."

"Aeva, I'm not the only one keeping secrets," Rowen said. "I was trying to protect you. General Altontaur isn't. He wants two things from you: the chip, and your uterus. The chip will give Ryths access to earth so they can have endless natural female uteri. In the meantime, he'll kill our baby growing in your belly and use your uterus to incubate his Ryth babies. Am I right, general?"

"It's a shame you can't understand the true reason for the chip," Altontaur said to Rowen, "and you are wrong with your twisted ways of thinking about our kind. We are an amiable race. Our kind is dying due to a rare viral attack on our females' reproductive system. We're in dire need of help and here you are making us out to be the enemy." In a gentler tone to Aeva, he said, "He's lied to you before. Do you trust him?"

Aeva put her hand on her flat stomach. There was no physical sign of a pregnancy yet, but it was as if something finally made sense to her. "I don't trust him," she answered.

"Turn off the forcefield," Altontaur said to the guard standing next to the shut-off button. The guard quickly did as he was told. "Bring him to me." The two guards took

Rowen by his arms and brought him in front of the general. "What shall I do with you?"

"Put me in one of the pods to Earth. I'll be out of your hair for good," Rowen said.

"You think Earth wants you?"

"I'm sure they'd rather have me than you—"

A sucker punch to Rowen's stomach from the general winded him and he gasped for air. The pain was so intense, he could barely make a sound. The guards let go of his arms and the general swung an uppercut, sending Rowen flying backwards hitting the ground with a thud. The general laughed while Rowen folded into a ball and bellowed an agonizing sound.

"Pick him up," Altontaur demanded the officers. They followed promptly and held Rowen by his arms. There was no strength left in him and the guards weren't strong enough to hold him upright, so his legs dragged behind. "Get on your feet, captain."

It took Rowen thirty seconds to stand upright and just as he was upright the general's fist came flying. He tried to duck but didn't move fast enough and was hit on the side of his nose. Blood sprayed and oozed into his mouth. The general pulled back his fist for another punch. It hit Rowen in the jaw, and he fell to the side, moaning. The general grabbed Rowen by the shirt and slammed him against the wall, punching him some more.

"I thought you were against brutality," Aeva said, remaining calm.

At her words, Altontaur stopped punching Rowen and rubbed his bruised and bloodied knuckles. "Are you worried I'll kill him?"

"I'm not worried about you killing him. I never knew Ryths were so...violent."

The general looked away from her, still rubbing his knuckles. "I regret you having to see this. You are right, we are not a brutal species, and violence doesn't run in our blood. I promise this won't happen again. You see, Teschner has been a thorn in my side. He's been an itch I can't seem to get rid of, and I've let myself go. I'll report him to the Federation and let them deal with him."

"Aeva, no. D...don't believe anything he s-says." Rowen mumbled, then moaned out a breath from the pain. She looked at him, but her expression was blank.

"Have any last words for him?" the general asked.

Still facing Rowen, she said, "You can rot in your own blood, you bastard."

The general smiled. "I'm starting to like you, Aeva."

When Aeva and the general left, the guards threw Rowen back in his cell. He went unconscious and dreamed he was on Pfore and Ryth soldiers were coming after him and a very pregnant Aeva. They were in a tunnel running from the soldiers and Aeva had to stop to catch her breath. "We need to keep moving!" he yelled at her.

"Go on without me," she said, breathing rapidly. "I can't run anymore." A tear from her eye came down her cheek and he wiped it away with his thumb. He wanted to carry her, but he'd been shot in the arm and wouldn't be able to lift her.

"There's no time. Let's go." She refused to move and leaned against the wall. He put his hands on her shoulders, and through gritted teeth said, "I'm not leaving you."

Her right hand reached out and squeezed his left arm. "Rowen...Rowen...Rowen..." she repeated.

He shook awake and there, next to him on her knees, was Aeva. "I'm not leaving you!" he shouted, pulling her to him for a tight hug. She was taken aback and froze. Within seconds, he came to his senses. Realizing he was in a dream, he apologized. "I didn't mean to—" he began, releasing her. "I was dreaming."

"You have to get up."

"What are you doing here?"

"I've disabled security for a little bit. I need you to help me."

"So much for rotting in my own blood, huh?" He tried to smile.

She bit down on her lip and scowled. That shut him up real quick. She reached over on the bench where she had set a damp cloth and wiped the dried and crusted blood from his face. His left eye was swollen and there was a cut on the left side of his lip which had also crusted. She had also brought a canister of water and handed it to him. "It's water infused with vitamins and some other ingredients. Should give you most of your strength back faster than normal."

"Where'd you find this stuff?"

"Dr. DeShevell gave them to me."

He sat up, took the canister, and gulped the water down. While he was doing that, she reached behind her back and pulled out a photon laser gun. "Whoa! How'd you get that photon blaster?"

"I stole it from an officer. I don't know how to use it so it's for you." She handed the gun to him. He took it and held it firmly.

"This thing can liquefy a person in seconds."

"I figured you'd know a thing or two about it."

"Haven't held one of these babies for a while." Aeva didn't reply. She simply held his arm and helped him to a standing position. "They took the chip out?"

"It's out."

"I must have slept through the morning—the chip!"

Dr. DeShevell must have waited for him and realizing he wasn't going to show up, surrendered it to Altontaur. Either that or she never meant to give it to him.

"You slept through the whole day, and you'd still be sleeping if I didn't wake you."

"Where's the chip?"

"With the pods."

"The pods?" Before she could answer, he remembered she was with child and said, "The baby—did you?"

"Abort? No," she said without looking at him. "We need to get to the pods now. In order to turn on the pods and for security purposes, the stations require a combination of the chip and my fingerprint. Krane did a test run a few hours ago but didn't release the pods or send anyone to Earth yet. He wanted to make sure they worked. The chip can't be removed from where it's been put. He set the launch for eight hours. That was four hours ago."

"Good. We have time." He stood up with her help. "I see he has you using his name."

"He prefers it."

A slight jealously filled Rowen and stopped him from inquiring any further about the general. At the same time, he had an urge to speak his heart. "Before we go...I...I want to say, I love you."

"Dr. DeShevell warned me. The infused water will make you say stupid things."

"It's not the water."

"Rowen. We don't have time for this."

"Remember in Judenome, you asked if I loved you? Well I—"

"Not now, okay? We need to get out of here."

The infused water was working quickly. Rowen felt the

effects. His proximities tingled and he felt strengthened. The fuzziness from the concussion on his head cleared up and he could think straight again. His bruises were still there but they were not as obvious.

"I have to tell you something else—"

"Tell me when we get to Earth."

He clenched his jaw. "Alright."

They took an elevator to an area below the main deck where unused fighter jets and smaller transport ships were docked. A few turns right and left and they came upon the exit pods. The oval pods were lined against the far wall running the length of the wall. Aeva walked up to the pod closest to them. All the pods were encased behind a security glass that could only be opened using the palm on the security pad. She walked down the length of the wall until she came to the pod at the end. There, she put her palm on the security pad and the glass slid open.

"This is it," Rowen said, looking at her.

She looked from the pod to him then back to the pod. They both stood there a few seconds staring at the small area within the pod. The pods were single seats with a navigation panel in the front. On the seats were a single folded suit and a helmet with a full-face mask. "Let me open this one," she said while walking toward the next pod. Before she touched the security pad to the second pod, an alarm sounded. It was a loud buzzing repeating sound. The lights went out and green emergency lights came on.

He grabbed for the suit and helmet in the first pod and handed it to her. "Put on the suit."

She opened the second pod before taking the suit and helmet. "Put yours on too."

"I should keep watch while you put yours on. I'll put mine on after you. Quickly!"

She swiftly dressed in the suit and zipped the front. He helped her with the helmet making sure it was secured correctly, then helped her into the pod to make sure she was all set. Once inside, he punched a few keys on the navigation pad. The pod's engine came on. "You're ready to go."

"I can't believe this is happening. I'll see you on Earth," she said with hope in her eyes.

"There they are!" a guard shouted a few yards away, pointing in their direction. The guards rushed toward them.

Rowen pulled out the photon blaster and aimed at the closest guard who was fifty yards away. He shot the guard and the guard turned into a puddle of liquid. Two other guards were right behind the liquified guard and slipped on the liquid, both tumbling down. Rowen shot them before they had any chance of getting up.

The commotion caught Aeva's attention and she saw Rowen liquify the two guards who had slipped. She feared he wouldn't make it to his pod, so she opened the door to her pod and stepped out. "Rowen, get suited!"

From around the corner where the guards were liquified came General Altontaur. "Well, well. An attempt escape I see."

Rowen held the photon blaster at the general. "Don't move," he told the general. To Aeva, he said, "Get back in your pod."

"Not without you."

"I won't be coming."

"Then I won't be going."

"Don't be foolish. Leave now."

"I'm not going without you."

Rowen looked at Aeva for one last time, pausing a moment to remember her. "All right. I'll be right behind you. I promise."

He turned toward the general who hadn't moved, then glanced at Aeva again. She had slipped into her seat and clicked the door-close button. As soon as the door closed the engine revved up louder. Within seconds, the pod detached from its holding spot and launched into space.

"She's safe now," the general said. "You got what you wanted, now put the blaster down, and we'll talk."

Rowen kept his blaster on the general.

"You wouldn't shoot a dying race now, would you?"

Rowen clicked the photon gun one notch lower to lower the photon emission then shot the general's right leg.

Altontaur's leg, up to his knee, liquefied. He screamed in agony, tumbling to the ground. "You'll pay for this!" he shouted in anguish. Blood began to seep out from above his knee.

"I don't think so," Rowen said before ramping up the blaster and firing it on each of the pods. "I want you to see how you'll never reach Earth. Not you. Not your species. Not ever." After the pods were liquified, Rowen turned the blaster back to the general whose face had turned pale from blood loss.

"D-don't shoot me. I'll give you anything you want, anything," Altontaur begged. "Please, anything."

Rowen thought on it. What could he want that would be worth all that the general put him through? The general took his wife from him, removed him from his position, nearly aborted his unborn child, kept him from being with the new love of his life, and now he was here with nothing to him, once again.

"There is one thing I want," Rowen said.

"Yes, say it. It's all yours."

"I want never to see you again." He ramped the photon

blaster to the max emission and shot. The general was liqui-fied to a clear puddle in seconds.

Rowen dropped the blaster and looked at the empty space where Aeva's pod had been. A mixture of anguish and relief fell over him and he slumped his shoulders, staring blankly at the floor. He would have married her if time had allowed it. She'll be a good mother to their child; there was no doubt about it.

"Rowen?"

The voice sounded familiar. He looked up and toward the puddles. Moving into view was his ex-wife with her right hand on the grip of her photon blaster tucked in a side holster.

"Maya," he said, more in confusion than surprise.

"What are you doing here?" Her hands still on the blaster.

He wanted to ask her the same but then his eyes drifted to her protruding belly and he remembered she wasn't the person he once knew. She was dressed in a loose-fitting satin-sequined gown. Her hair was tied up in a bun with wispy ringlets down the side of her face. She looked beau-tiful even with the general's baby growing in her.

He had nothing to say to her.

"Guards will be here soon," she warned him.

"I don't care."

"I can stop them."

He didn't say anything but kept his eyes on hers.

The swift sound of boots became louder as the guards got closer.

"Rowen..." Unshed tears lined Maya's big gray eyes. "I'm sorry..." She looked as though she wanted to say more but knew it wasn't the time or place.

He turned from her to the one pod he hadn't shot. When

he glanced back at her, she was gone. He could hear her talking to the guards down the hall but couldn't hear what was being said. Within a few seconds the sound of boots slowly faded, and all was quiet except for the natural hum of the ship.

ACKNOWLEDGMENTS

I'd like to thank my editor, J. Benkers. I wouldn't have done it without your expertise and patience. Many thanks to Bruce Landay and Christopher Hageney for your excellent feedback during the early stages of Aeva. Your time and dedication were truly appreciated. I'd also like to thank the beta readers who offered their honest opinions and insights. It meant the world to me.

ABOUT THE AUTHOR

Tori C. Lore is an author of science fiction. This is Tori's first book.

 facebook.com/toricloreauthor

CPSIA information can be obtained
at www.ICGtesting.com
Printed in the USA
LVHW032121040321
680568LV00008B/113

9 781954 834002